THE 39 CLUES

"Dan could not see the future, but one thing seemed absolutely crystal clear: If Amy died because of this decision, he would never be able to live with himself."

UNSTOPPABLE

FLASHPOINT

GORDON KORMAN

SCHOLASTIC INC.

For Rossana

Library of Congress Control Number: 2014935050

ISBN 978-0-545-52147-5

10 9 8 7 6 5 4 3 2 1   14 15 16 17 18/0

Bald Eagle p. 18: © escova/Shutterstock; Jonah Wizard p. 218:
Ken Karp for Scholastic; Poster Texture p. 218: CG Textures;
All other image work by Charice Silverman for Scholastic
Book design by Charice Silverman

First edition, September 2014

Printed in China 62

Scholastic US: 557 Broadway • New York, NY 10012
Scholastic Canada: 604 King Street West • Toronto, ON M5V 1E1
Scholastic New Zealand Limited: Private Bag 94407 • Greenmount, Manukau 2141
Scholastic UK Ltd.: Euston House • 24 Eversholt Street • London NW1 1DB

CHAPTER 1

Dan Cahill awoke from a bad dream only to find himself in the midst of a worse one.

Images of the past twelve hours flashed like a rapid-fire slide show of horror inside his brain: a madman with the power of the US presidency nearly within his grasp; Pony—ally and friend—killed, trying to rescue Dan . . .

And Amy . . .

Tears blurred his vision just as it returned to him. His sister was dying, a timer literally ticking her life away.

He blinked the moisture from his eyes. He was tied to the armrests of a leather airline seat. Dan had spent enough time aboard Jonah Wizard's Gulfstream to recognize the luxury interior of a private jet. Only this one didn't belong to Dan's celebrity cousin. . . .

"He's awake!" exclaimed a gruff, unpleasant voice.

Galt Pierce was striding down the aisle. He was blond, brawny, and ripped—*unnaturally* ripped. His older sister, Cara, was right behind him, slimmer, feminine, but also muscular. Which meant this was the plane of J. Rutherford Pierce, head of Founders Media, billionaire, tycoon, megalomaniac, and the madman who wanted Dan dead.

Cara untied Dan's right arm and handed him a cup of water. Thirsty as he was, Dan couldn't resist tossing it back in her face. It was a pointless thing to do — but also deeply satisfying. *For Pony*, he thought, hatred flooding his soul. *And for Amy!* If it hadn't been for Cara's father, Amy never would have taken the serum that had started her on a death clock.

"You little —" Galt raised his hand, ready to bring it down hard across Dan's cheek.

Cara grabbed his wrist. "Don't!"

He stared at his sister. "You're letting him get away with that?"

"You think I want to?" Cara demanded, the water dripping down her cheeks and nose. "But if you break his jaw, how's he going to tell us what we need to know?"

"What you need to know?" Dan was instantly alert. Outside the window of the jet, the wings dipped, bringing a sliver of the Central American rain forest into view. Dan had felt it in the aircraft's motion, but his brain had been unable to process the information until now. "We're circling! We're still over Guatemala!"

"So?" Galt snapped.

"So you were waiting for me to wake up! You *need* me!"

"Don't flatter yourself, Dan," Cara said coolly. "We know exactly what you and your sister have been up to—"

"Our dad decoded your ratty old book!" Galt interrupted.

Dan gasped in mock horror. "You mean he figured out our secret recipe for potato salad?"

Galt howled his outrage, but Cara put a hand on his arm. Something about the gesture reminded Dan of Amy. Normally, such acts of big-sisterliness annoyed him to no end. But right then, he ached to see Amy, to know she was okay. Only, that would have meant she'd been captured along with him. And besides, she wasn't okay. She was the polar opposite of okay.

"There's an antidote to the serum," Cara told Dan. "That's what you and Amy have been working on. We want to know how much progress you've made."

"Yeah, I'd be wondering about it, too, if I were you." Dan sat back with a smirk. "Good luck with that."

There was a rattling sound as a stainless steel rolling cart was pushed down the aisle by a Pierce employee. *Goon* might have been a better word. J. Rutherford Pierce's henchmen looked like adult versions of Galt and Cara, and like Pierce himself. Big, muscular, enhanced—glowing, almost. It was all artificial. The key was the same secret that had made the Cahills the most influential, successful, and powerful family in history. The 39 Clues—a serum with thirty-nine ingredients that gave a person nearly superhuman strength, genius, creativity, and cunning. Pierce had gotten hold of a modified version of the stuff and was feeding it to his staff, his family, and even himself. It had rendered him—and everybody around him—virtually unstoppable. That was why Dan; his sister, Amy; and their companions were risking everything on this quest—to assemble the ingredients of an ancient antidote to Gideon Cahill's formula. It was the only way to thwart Pierce's dangerous ambitions.

The attendant plucked a hypodermic syringe off the tray and held it up to the light. It was filled with clear liquid. Panicked, Dan tried to struggle, but Galt grabbed his free arm and pinned it to the seat.

A mewl of desperation escaped Dan as the needle drew nearer.

"Wimp." Galt smirked. "If we wanted to kill you, you'd already be dead."

"It's sodium pentothal," his sister added. "Truth serum."

Dan knew the sting of the needle and braced himself for the onslaught to come. But instead of blinding pain or nausea, he experienced a flood of warmth and well-being. Warning bells went off somewhere inside his head.

Stop feeling good, stupid! That's how the truth drug works! You get too comfortable and spill your guts!

To counteract the effect—*fight it, fight it!*—he forced his mind onto unpleasant thoughts. For a Cahill, there were always a lot of options. The death of his parents

THE 39 CLUES

4

in a fire when he was only four; the sight of poor Pony, his eyes wide with terror, dropping from a helicopter to a violent end on the rain forest floor. And most painful of all, the last days he'd spent with Amy.

Amy had saved his life, but in order to do it, she'd had to take the serum. Not the modified version that Pierce was using to dose his people, but the real thing — Gideon Cahill's five-hundred-year-old recipe, pure and strong. The real serum produced extraordinary results almost instantly. But no one had ever survived longer than a week after taking it. Now it was doubly urgent to complete the antidote. Amy's life depended on it.

Dan pulled himself up short. *Did I say that out loud or just think it?* He realized uneasily that he couldn't be sure. It was the injection working on his mind.

"And how many ingredients have you collected so far?" Cara probed.

"What?" The sodium pentothal was making it impossible to distinguish between thoughts and speech. "Did I say antidote? I meant *anecdote* — you know, like a funny story —"

Galt muscled into his view. "The ingredients — do you have them all?"

"I have no idea what you're talking about," Dan announced, pleased that his resistance seemed to be working now. Of the seven antidote components mentioned in the diary of his ancestor, Olivia Cahill, Amy and Dan had already acquired three. Other Cahill sources around the globe had come up with three more. That left just one remaining.

In horror, Dan heard the sound of his own voice. He was *talking*, and Cara and Galt were nodding and listening! He tried to add, "Forget that! I'm lying!" but the words just wouldn't come out.

"Confirm the location of the final ingredient," Galt persisted.

The antidote had been assembled from the ancient wisdom of seven lost cities. The last of these — the one Dan must not reveal — was located in modern Cambodia, in the ancient Khmer civilization of Angkor.

"Anger?" Galt was no scholar. "Dad said it was in Cambodia."

"Not *Anger*," Cara corrected. "*Angkor* — and it *is* in Cambodia. Angkor was one of the most developed societies of the ancient world!"

No! Dan was in agony. *I spilled that, too, although the Pierces seemed to know it already. I'm a living, breathing Wikipedia!* He had to stop himself before he gave up any more information. But how? The injection made it impossible to keep anything secret.

Galt was like a bloodhound. "What's the ingredient, and where do we find it in this Angkor place?"

Dan bit down on his lip until he tasted blood. He had to get out of this, but the enemy was *himself* and the chemical inside him that was turning him into a blabbermouth. Then he spotted the bottle on the rolling tray. *Chloroform*, read the label.

Knockout drops!

He pulled his hand free of Galt's grip and grabbed for the bottle. In the ensuing struggle, the contents spilled onto Dan's shirt. Crowing in triumph, he buried his face in the wet fabric and breathed the strong solvent odor. With a great sense of accomplishment, he felt himself slipping away.

You can't talk if you're unconscious!

He slumped in the seat, useless to them now.

Galt slapped Dan's face, but the prisoner did not stir. The sharp contact filled Galt with an exhilaration he wouldn't have believed possible. Finally, he was a part of his father's plans! Not just posing for father-and-son pictures, but taking action. He was a real Piercer now, a soldier for the cause!

"Wake up!" Energized, he reared back to strike another blow, but his sister grabbed his wrist.

"It's no use," she told him. "He's out like a light."

Galt turned to the man with the syringe. "Toss him out the door."

"Are you crazy?" Cara exploded. "We're at fifteen thousand feet!"

Galt glared at his sister. Where did she get off contradicting him? "He's already told us what we need to know."

"Think, Galt—this is huge! An antidote in Cahill

hands — it's the one thing that could wreck Dad's plans."

"All the more reason for *him* to go skydiving without a parachute!" growled Galt, indicating the unmoving Dan.

She shook her head. "I've heard he has a photographic memory — that means he can tell us everything the Cahills have seen and done. The kid has more uses than a Swiss Army knife. We're not going to harm a single hair on his head."

Galt opened his mouth to overrule her, but bit back the angry words. He looked around the cabin at his father's hired muscle. There was something in their expressions and body language that told him they were tuned in to his sister's orders, not his own.

When had *that* happened? *He* had always been Dad's favorite, and he'd grown up believing he'd be Dad's heir. Sure, Cara would be entitled to her share of the money. Yet the business, the *power* — J. Rutherford Pierce was going to be president of the United States soon. And even that was only the first step in Dad's master plan. . . .

"Tie the prisoner back in his seat," Cara ordered the henchmen. "I'm going to talk to the pilot about a flight plan to Cambodia."

Galt burned with resentment. Those should have been *his* lines.

The Pierce siblings worked for their father, but that didn't necessarily mean they were on the same side.

CHAPTER 2

The Jeep hit an exposed root, jouncing eighteen inches straight up and nearly launching the four occupants into the jungle underbrush.

Instead of slowing down, Amy Cahill stomped on the gas, coaxing even more speed out of the rickety four-wheeler.

"Everybody okay?" called Jake Rosenbloom from the passenger seat, hanging on to the roll bar.

"Barely," groaned Ian Kabra. "I nearly lost my computer, not to mention my lunch."

"Ponyrific," Jake replied soberly, using Pony's nickname for his custom laptop. "It's all we have left of — him."

The brilliant Pony had built the machine himself, using components from some of the best computers anywhere. It was a magnificent machine, but it could never replace the magnificent friend who'd been taken from them.

Another bump sent passengers bouncing around the Jeep.

"I thought the rental agent said this was a good road," Ian complained in his clipped British accent.

"In actuality," put in Atticus Rosenbloom, Jake's younger brother, "she never said it was *good*. She just said it was better than the roads in Honduras."

"You asked me to research the Tonle Sap water snake," Ian persisted. "With all this tossing about, I can't find the T key. Not even Pony could work under these conditions. Do slow down, Amy!"

Amy let up a little on the accelerator. Thanks to her serum-boosted acuity of vision, she had actually watched Pony's grip on the chopper's skid fail, sending him plunging to his death. Loyal Pony—who wasn't even a Cahill—had offered his digital cowboy skills to their quest. And the cost had been his life.

Amy's grip tightened on the steering wheel. That was the helicopter that had flown off with Dan. For all she knew, at this very moment, her younger brother was being tortured.

For all she knew, he was as dead as Pony.

To keep from screaming, she pressed harder on the accelerator, and the Jeep leaped forward, rattling and rocking along the dirt road.

"As much as I hate to agree with Ian," Jake ventured, "this is crazy driving. We're not going to be able to help anybody if we hit a tree."

"We're not going to hit a tree," returned Amy through clenched teeth. "I'm in total control of this car."

"Good to know," Ian said smoothly, "because I left my spleen about twelve kilometers back."

"But, Amy," Jake persisted, "We need to talk about *why* you're in total control of this car—*why* you can drive like a NASCAR champion on a road meant for ox carts."

"There's nothing to talk about," Amy snapped. "I took the serum. Stop worrying. I'm fine!"

She *was* fine. Better than fine, and not just because the serum was making her faster and stronger with every passing hour. Her thinking was clear. She could plan strategic moves and countermoves almost to infinity. Her eyesight was amazing, her hearing acute, her reaction time virtually instantaneous. She had no superpowers—she couldn't lift locomotives or fly through the air. Yet her natural capabilities were enhanced to the nth degree.

No sooner had this thought crossed her soaring mind than the pinkie of her left hand began to twitch slightly against the wheel. Under normal circumstances, she would not even have noticed it. But in her heightened state of acuity, she understood that this tiny spasm represented the beginning of the end. It was Amy's future—the loss of control; the organ failure; the terrible, painful conclusion. The serum was glorious—until it wasn't. And that, apparently, happened very quickly. The stuff could burn out a human being inside of a week. Amy would suffer the same fate if they couldn't come up with the antidote.

How crazy was that? She'd never felt better in her life — and she was dying.

Suddenly, an enormous logging truck roared out of the trees, looming above, almost upon them, its broad cab hogging most of the road. Before any of them could shout, "Amy, look out!" she was on it. Her reaction was lightning fast — the instant her eyes identified the danger, her hands were moving the steering wheel. She found the path that hadn't been there milliseconds earlier, squeezing through an impossible gap with mere inches to spare. Then they were back on the road, full speed ahead, as if nothing had happened.

For a few breathless seconds, no one spoke. Before, there hadn't been enough time to scream; now it was no longer necessary.

"Don't take this the wrong way, Amy," Ian managed at last. "But at the moment, I'm really glad you swallowed that serum."

No normal driver could have avoided that truck. Gideon's formula may have been a death sentence, but it had just saved all their lives.

At that moment, the Jeep suffered one tremendous jolt before the ride leveled off, becoming not only smoother but quieter as well.

Jake was instantly alert. "What happened? What did we hit?"

"Pavement," supplied Atticus, daring to look over the side. "We must be getting close to Guatemala City."

With the better road conditions, Ian was able to

return to his research on Pony's laptop. "The Tonle Sap water snake," he reported. "Scientific name: *Enhydris longicauda*. A slightly venomous colubrid snake native to the Tonle Sap, Cambodia's Great Lake. It's a close relative of the sea leopard snake, the rice paddy snake, and the Kapuas mud snake."

"'Slightly venomous'?" Atticus repeated. "What does that mean—when it bites you, you only get a little bit dead?"

"If you think about it," mused Amy, "the venom can't be deadly or it wouldn't work as part of the antidote. It's not much of a cure if it kills everybody who takes it."

"All the colubrid snakes are slightly venomous," Ian continued his report. "There are nearly two thousand different species of them. And—uh-oh—"

"What is it?" asked Jake.

"The Red List of Threatened Species lists ours as vulnerable. That's only one step better than endangered. Apparently, this part of Cambodia is big on crocodile farming, and the Tonle Sap water snake was a widely used crocodile food. The only problem is the crocs can eat them faster than the snakes can reproduce."

Amy frowned. "Five hundred years ago, when the antidote was created, they were probably all over the place."

"That won't help us *now*," Jake put in nervously. "We need that venom!"

"Relax." Amy's reply sounded more like an order.

"We got whiskers from an extinct leopard; we can find venom from a threatened snake." She glanced in the rearview mirror to find a quizzical expression on Ian's fine features. "What's the problem?"

"I think Pony's computer is trying to tell me something," Ian replied. He swiveled the screen toward Atticus. "You see that? 'Code A'? What do you think it means?"

Atticus shrugged. He was an eleven-year-old genius, but his area of expertise was dead languages and ancient civilizations. Computer technology was several centuries too recent for him.

All at once, Amy stomped on the brake with every ounce of power in her serum-enhanced muscles. The other three were nearly pitched out of the vehicle as the Jeep lurched to a halt behind a stopped bus. Amy stared in amazement. Less than an hour ago, they had been traveling through isolated rain forest terrain. Now the buildings of Guatemala City were clearly visible in the distance, and the Cahill team was stalled in the largest traffic jam any of them had ever seen.

Thousands of screaming fans packed the broad Avenida Simón Bolívar. The mayor was in attendance, along with a gaggle of local VIPs, most of them with their young daughters in tow. Camera phones waved and flashed. So great was the demand to upload pictures that the Guatemalan servers for Facebook and Twitter crashed. The line for autographs measured in kilometers. The crowd noise was an uninterrupted roar, punctuated by applause. It was an absolute mob scene.

Or, in the life of pop star Jonah Wizard, just another day.

"Wassup, yo?" Jonah greeted the next girl in line, an adoring preteen who didn't seem to speak a word of English. Wielding a fat Sharpie, he scribbled a quick signature on her CD, and another on her arm when she held it out to him. "Thanks for coming out. 'Preciate the support!"

Standing behind the autographing table, Broderick Wizard, Jonah's father, wore a scowl as he texted on his BlackBerry. "I have to tell you, Jonah, I don't get it. When you said you had to drop out of the public eye, I was okay with that. Then, six months in, when you told me to set up an appearance, I never asked why. I just made it happen. But I'm asking you now — why did it have to be *here*?"

Jonah motioned to the legions of fans, which only made them scream louder. "Look around, Pops. Can't you feel the *love*?"

His father was unconvinced. "You get love in New York. Also London, Paris, Tokyo, anywhere. But you said it had to be Guatemala and it had to be today. Why?"

Jonah had an excellent answer to this question — although not one he could give to his father. The Cahill team had to get to Jonah's private jet, but Pierce had substantial assets hunting for them. A group of kids could stay hidden, but not a Gulfstream G6 parked on a runway. The goons would stake out the airport and open fire on anybody who approached the plane.

There was only one solution. Pierce didn't dare attack when there were people around. And drawing a crowd happened to be Jonah's specialty.

He surveyed the street up and down, his famous eyes coming to focus on an open Jeep stalled in the traffic snarl. He might have failed to notice the three young passengers, but the driver was something else. She fairly glowed with strength and vitality. It was natural to pick her out of a crowd of thousands. He felt a stab of dread as he remembered what it was that made his cousin Amy stand out.

He got up from his chair and took a flying leap off the stage.

"Jonah!" his father howled in dismay.

There was never any danger. Jonah knew that his sea of admirers would catch him before he hit the pavement.

Broderick Wizard was at the edge of the platform, gawking at his son. "What are you doing?"

"It's all good, Pops!" Jonah called back at him. "But you're going to have to fly home commercial! I need the jet!"

By that time, the Guatemala City police had reached him and were clearing a path through the throng. High-fiving and *wassup*-ing all the way, Jonah led them to the Jeep and swung himself aboard. "Good timing," he approved. "The Wiz was getting writer's cramp."

"Real smart, Jonah," Jake scolded. "Who knows how long we'll be stuck here. Pierce will have time to see us on TMZ and send half his army after us."

Jonah addressed his police escort. "Need you homeys to get us to the airport. You know, *el runway-o—*"

"*Aeropuerto,*" supplied Atticus.

Nodding their understanding, the police officers organized themselves into two lines, opening up a path for the Jeep. Just outside the throng, a cavalcade of motorcycle cops surrounded the Cahills for their ride.

"Those goons are going to have a heart attack when we drive up to the plane with half the Guatemalan police force!" Atticus crowed.

"That's how I do," Jonah acknowledged modestly.

His fans cheered, waved, and threw flowers as he passed among them, perched on the tailgate.

"Later, Guatemala City!" bellowed the famous voice. "Gotta hop! *Adiós,* yo!" He grinned down at his cowed Jeep-mates. "Anybody need a lift to Cambodia?"

A battery of spotlights fixed on J. Rutherford Pierce.

Technically, he had not yet declared that he was running for president. But it was the worst-kept secret on the planet. Everybody knew he was bound for the Oval Office. What was not general knowledge was that the White House was only a small part of his overall plan.

But first things first—this rally in New York's Central Park. CNN estimated the crowd at upward of half a million. That was a lot of eyes on Pierce as he strutted onstage before an enormous banner that read:

It was the slogan of the Patriotist Party—the organization that was poised to rocket Pierce to the highest office in the country.

"I've got nothing against international cooperation—so long as America calls all the shots!" he harangued the audience, who cheered even louder. "One nation, one vote may be fine at the UN, but I don't like those odds. We worked hard to get where we are, and now we're going broke buying things *we* invented from *foreign countries*! And our current president thinks that's just fine. Well, I say this land is—"

"Our land!" roared the crowd with a single voice that rose into the atmosphere.

As he basked in their adoration, a tremor caused his right leg to spasm. Determined not to show any weakness, he converted the involuntary shudder into a karate kick. The audience ate it up. It was almost like he was striking a blow against America's enemies.

Once the election campaign started, all he had to do was let the current president talk about being global citizens, one country among many, a whole international community, blah, blah, blah. Then a series of small nuclear explosions would rock several far-flung cities on distant continents, and the voters would face a simple choice: bet America's future on a crumbling world order of dangerous and unstable foreigners, or take control in a manner befitting the greatest nation that had ever been.

No one would ever find out that the atomic blasts had been arranged by Pierce himself—at least, not before Election Day. By the time the truth came out—if it ever did—J. Rutherford Pierce would be established as more than just a president. He would be a dictator, commanding a United Planet Earth.

But first things first.

"My fellow Americans, I stand before you a humble man, grateful for your loyalty and support. And now I'd like to introduce you to the woman whose love and guidance keeps me humble — my beautiful wife, Debi Ann."

Debi Ann stepped out from the wings and took his arm. If the crowd of loyal Piercers noticed how bland, ordinary, and, well, *old* she looked, it did not come across in the tumultuous ovation. She was actually six years *younger* than her husband, but Debi Ann had not been receiving the "protein shakes" dosed with serum, like the rest of her family.

Not her fault, Pierce reminded himself. It had been his decision to keep at least one Pierce non-fabulous for ordinary Americans to relate to. And anyway, no serum could do anything for Debi Ann's colorless personality. She wouldn't crackle if you put four thousand volts through her. Face it, marrying her had been one of his bad decisions — and he had an attic full of her homemade teddy bears to prove it.

One day — after all his plans had come to fruition — he would have to find a painless way to put her out to pasture. But that was in the future. Presidential candidates had perfect marriages to perfect women. He embraced her fondly. The gesture concealed another tremor, this one in his right arm. The audience ate it up.

He experienced an if-only moment as he remembered the girl he'd really wanted to marry, the exquisite Hope Cahill, the one true love of his life. Of course, Debi Ann Starling was a Cahill, too, but as different from Hope as marbles from diamonds. A lot of men would have pined away, but not Pierce. He had channeled his disappointment into a far more productive emotion: bitter hatred of the woman who had rejected him. Hope was gone now, dead in a tragic fire. So the target of all that ill will was her two children, Amy and Dan. He had already used his media empire to ruin their reputations. And he would not stop until they joined their parents in death. It was not the primary objective of Pierce's grand plan, merely a pleasant fringe benefit.

Those kids had no idea that their mother had spurned J. Rutherford Pierce. But they would pay the ultimate price for it anyway.

Halfway to her lips, the crystal glass shattered in Amy's hands. Cranberry juice ran in rivulets down her arm, followed by a darker red. Blood.

"Chillax with the Waterford," Jonah groaned. "My bank's not what it used to be since I stopped touring."

Jake was already by Amy's side with a first aid kit. "You've got to ease up, Amy," he urged, dabbing at her palm with a gauze pad soaked in disinfectant.

"You don't know your own strength anymore."

"I'm fine," Amy said irritably. "I think the serum boosts clotting factor, too. See? It's already stopped bleeding."

The group was aboard Jonah's jet, heading westward across the vast Pacific Ocean en route to Cambodia.

"I'm not just talking to hear the sound of my own voice," Jake persisted. "What do I have to do to make you appreciate the kind of danger you're in — tie you to a chair?"

"In actuality," Atticus put in, "the whole group of us probably couldn't tie her to a chair."

"It's not just strength," Amy tried to explain. "It's everything. I can hear the pilot flicking switches in the cockpit, and see every tiny flaw in the fabric of Jonah's shirt —"

The star snorted indignantly. "Yo, cuz! I bought this on Rodeo Drive! Are you saying the Wiz got ripped off?"

Amy went on as if he hadn't spoken. "My reactions are instant. If you show me a chessboard, I can see thirty moves ahead."

"You might not *have* thirty moves," Jake said bitterly. "You've got seven days, tops, and three of them are already gone!"

An explosion of light and color went off in her head, the grand finale of a Fourth of July fireworks display. The hallucinations were the flip side of the tremors. Her brain was seizing up, not just her body.

She sat down next to Ian, who was still hunched

over Pony's laptop.

"I'm still getting the Code A signal," he said, looking exhausted. "Do you think it's some kind of error message?"

Amy was doubtful. "There's no error Pony wouldn't have known how to fix. If there's a Code A, it's because he wanted it to be there." Her fingers danced across the keyboard at light speed. The monitor flickered once and displayed a map of the world, with a pulsing red dot at the center of the screen.

Ian sat forward, eyes wide. "A tracking beacon?"

Amy pointed to the dot, which was over the Pacific Ocean just off the Central American coastline. "Whatever he's tracking is headed for Asia."

Jake peered over her shoulder. "*We're* headed for Asia. Could that be *us*?"

"I see why his dizzying intellect appeals to you, Amy," Ian sniffed. "Naturally, Pony would track one of his own allies. Why didn't I think of it?"

"Ian has a point," said Amy. "The beacon must be on another plane, a couple of hundred miles ahead of us."

Jonah sat up. "You think it's Pierce's jet? How would that crew know where to go?"

"Pierce has Olivia's book," Amy concluded, "and the enhanced reasoning to figure out what it means."

Jonah was on the intercom in a flash. "Speed up, yo," he instructed. "I guess what I'm trying to say is: Follow that plane!"

CHAPTER 4

When Dan next saw the light of day, he was still tied to the seat in Pierce's jet. Something felt different, though. . . .

There was no airplane movement. They were on the ground.

He was still fuzzy from the chloroform. Could they be in Cambodia already? Surely he hadn't been out for that long.

Two figures gradually came into focus — Cara and Galt.

"He's awake," noted Galt. "Let's continue the interrogation." He sounded eager.

Cara stepped into the aisle in front of him. "I'll tighten his bonds so he can't get away."

Her brother snorted. "That shrimp couldn't bust out of a wet paper bag."

Dan swallowed a retort. The last thing he wanted to do was give Galt any additional motivation. The kid was already pounding his fist into his palm. His knuckles looked enormous.

Cara began to work on the rope around Dan's left wrist. "Do you want to have to tell Dad we lost him? We're not in the air, Galt. If he gets loose, he could make a run for it . . ."

Bewildered, Dan sat back and took in the situation. As Cara Pierce continued to lecture her brother on the importance of tightening the knots, she was actually *loosening* them! In fact, the ropes were now so slack, he was pretty sure he could slip out of them any time he wanted.

". . . all he'd have to do is pop the main door. And how hard is that? You remove the panel, pull down the lever . . ."

Dan was stunned. Was he reading this correctly? Pierce's own daughter was providing detailed instructions on how he could get away. She was either completely stupid or she *wanted* him to escape!

He decided to take a chance. His lips formed the word: *When?*

Her reply was barely a whisper: "You'll know."

The copilot appeared in the cockpit hatchway. "We're all refueled and ready for takeoff. I need everybody in their seats."

Galt scowled at Dan. "You're off the hook, Cahill, but not for long. As soon as we're airborne, I'm coming back to finish our *conversation*."

As the Pierce siblings strapped themselves into their private loungers in the front, Dan strained to see over his shoulder. The three goons sat around a small table in the aft part of the cabin, scarfing sandwiches and playing cards. If this wasn't *you'll know*, then *you'll know* was never coming.

The fuel truck backed away and the jet began to taxi toward the runway. Dan wriggled his arms free and plotted a mental course to the aircraft door. It was mid-cabin — not far from Galt, but behind him. And he and his sister were facing forward for departure.

The jet executed a small turn and began to roll forward, picking up speed. It was now or never.

Dan vaulted over a row of seats and reached the door in a single bound across the aisle. Cara's "instructions" did not let him down — the cover, the lever . . .

As the plastic panel hit the deck, a loud "Hey!" rang out behind him. Dan didn't hang around to find out which of the three goons had noticed him. He pushed with all his might. An alarm bell sounded in the cabin.

As the hatch came open, a blast of heavy tropical air nearly threw Dan back across the aisle. He bent his shoulder into the gale and fairly hurled himself outside. As his body toppled out of the moving jet, he bounced down the mini-stairway formed by the door. He hit the tarmac hard and went into a roll in an effort to get himself away from the aircraft. He leaped back up to his feet and broke into a limping run toward the large hangar complex about two hundred yards away. Surely there were people there — airport personnel and security guards, who wouldn't let him be kidnapped or worse.

That was when he saw the other plane.

It was coming right at him, wheels down, about to land on the runway the Pierce jet had just crossed. Its nose was so close that he could see the horrified face of the pilot behind the cockpit glass.

There was nothing Dan could do but drop flat, hug the blacktop, and pray. The Gulfstream roared in, its heavy tires passing just a few feet over his prone body. He felt the hot backwash of the engines, accompanied by an overwhelming suction. Then he was airborne, wrenched from his purchase on the pavement like a tiny bug pulled by the force of a vacuum cleaner.

In horror, he watched the airstrip fall away as he was drawn higher and higher in a tug-of-war between jet power and gravity.

Wham! He slammed down against the runway with such violence that everything went dark and he was certain he was dead.

The skid of rubber on tarmac jarred him back to awareness, and his vision returned with the sight of the big landing gear touching down just beyond him.

Mind and body numb, acting on instinct alone, he dragged himself to his feet and sprinted for the cover of the hangar.

Far out at the edge of the runway, the Pierce plane aborted takeoff and lurched to a halt.

The copilot burst into the cabin. "Who blew that hatch?" He pulled up on the stairs, and the hydraulic-assist system shut and resealed the door.

"No!" roared Galt. "We have to pick up the Cahill kid!"

"Forget it!" Cara exclaimed. "Too many people saw what just happened. The whole airport crew and who-ever's on that other plane."

"People can be kept quiet," Galt spat.

"You want to take that risk?" his sister challenged, deliberately stalling so Dan could make his escape. "Our father is less than a week away from announcing his bid for president. If we create a scandal here, that could ruin everything."

"That kid on the loose is a *bigger* risk!" Galt threw back in her face. "I'm the one who understands Dad's plan! It's me he trusts the most!"

"You're operating on old information, little brother." Cara indicated the three goons. "Just ask them who they take their orders from."

The hired muscle looked from Pierce to Pierce, unsure of what their next move should be.

Dan ran and did not look back, knowing that even a second's hesitation could mean the difference between escape and recapture by the Pierces.

He left the tarmac, struggling through thigh-high

grass. His body ached—he was probably black and blue from his sudden departure from the moving aircraft. And his face throbbed from the jet wash. Not the agony of a burn, it just felt—hot. He'd been lucky—but only considering how close he'd come to being crushed like a bug by a landing plane.

Knees pumping to maintain speed, he took in the vast hangar complex that loomed ahead.

Dan was enough of a World War II buff to recognize *that* name. Midway was a tiny atoll about halfway across the Pacific Ocean. It was the site of one of the most famous battles of the war. *NAF* was short for *Naval Air Facility*. That explained why such an enormous airport seemed so broken-down and empty. Once a location of great strategic importance, it was now a tiny refueling station most modern jets didn't need. The two planes that had nearly done him in were probably the most traffic this place had seen in decades.

Back on the pavement, Dan sprinted for the building, scouting for a way in. The hangar doors were shut, but enough glass was missing that he was able to squeeze through what had once been a low window.

Inside was dark, dusty, and oppressively hot. The

space was cavernous and empty, not exactly a formula for good hiding places. The only cover was a corner area of tables and shelving units that might have once been part of a machine shop. He made for it, snatching up a crowbar to use as a weapon if worse came to worst. Galt and the goons may have been pounding serum like Gatorade, but not even that could make a guy strong enough to withstand a crowbar sandwich. As for Cara — the thought of her gave Dan pause. She had clearly helped him get away, but no one could be certain what her real motive might be. Until Dan knew for sure, Cara was still the enemy.

He ducked behind the tallest shelf, wielding the iron tool like a baseball bat. There he crouched, poised for action, listening for the footfalls of an approaching enemy. The only sound besides his own ragged breathing was the chirping and buzzing of the tropical insects. It was something he'd learned long ago during the search for the 39 Clues — no matter where you were, you were never far from something gross that wanted to bite you.

Outside, he heard a plane take off, but only one. He had no way of knowing if it was the Pierce jet or the one that had almost run him over.

Then he heard the footsteps. He tried to peek around the corner and accidentally knocked a few ball bearings off a shelf. The ringing of metal on concrete seemed unbelievably loud in the silence.

The intruder shuffled closer, heading straight for

his hiding place. Well, okay, if it had to be a fight, so be it. He hefted the crowbar and watched for the head to come into view. He could already make out a white shirt on the other side of the shelving unit. Just another few seconds . . .

Betting on the element of surprise, he leaped out and, like any good Red Sox fan, swung for the Green Monster at Fenway Park. Too late to pull back, he recognized the target of his home-run swing.

Amy!

Her hand shot forward at lightning speed, grabbed the iron bar, and plucked it out of his grasp like it was a drinking straw.

He threw his arms around her. "I didn't mean to hit you! I mean—I meant to hit you, but I didn't know it was you!"

Amy tightened her embrace. "The important thing is we've got you back."

"My ribs!" he rasped, and she loosened her grip. "You're getting crazy strong, Amy."

The euphoria of their reunion vanished as they both remembered the reason for her newfound might. These days, happiness could never be more than a fleeting impression before cold reality returned.

Amy tried to put on a brave face. "The serum's amazing—if it wasn't for the part where you drop dead."

Conflicting emotions surged through him: fear for his sister's life, chagrin at nearly braining her, relief at being rescued, joy at seeing Amy. Dan had resolved to walk away from this Cahill craziness as soon as the Pierce affair was over, but that calculation never quite worked where his sister was concerned. Ever since their parents' death, the bond between the two orphans had been almost scary. Sometimes it seemed as if they could read each other's minds. "How did you find me?"

"We were following Pierce's plane. So when our pilot said there was some idiot on the runway, I figured it was probably you." She hugged him back, choking with emotion. "How did you get away?"

"That's the weird part. Cara Pierce saved me. At least, she sprang my arms and made it really obvious what I had to do to get out of the plane. You think she wants to change sides?"

Amy stared at him. "Pierce's daughter? She'd never change sides! She was *born* on the wrong side."

"I know all that, Amy," Dan returned. "I also know what I saw."

"She'd have to turn against her family and everything she's been taught to believe since the day she was born," Amy insisted. "That's not the Cara Pierce who's been fighting us tooth and nail since all this began. What else happened on that plane?"

Dan hung his head. "I messed up. Galt shot me full of truth juice and I sang like Lady Gaga. I let everybody down."

"You didn't—"

He could not meet her eyes. "Pony sacrificed his life

for us, and I couldn't even keep my big mouth shut."

"You were drugged," Amy said sternly. "Besides, you didn't tell them anything Pierce didn't already know. He's got Olivia's book and more than enough brain-power to decode it. And if he can't figure something out, he's got the world's greatest hacker on his payroll."

"April May. I almost forgot about her — or him." The notorious computer genius represented herself as female, but online identities could be easily fabricated. "Amy, sometimes I think about what we're up against, and it's not fair! I mean, we might have been a match for April May when we still had Pony, but —" The words caught in his throat and he could say no more.

"I miss him, too," Amy whispered, squeezing his arm. "Now let's get back on the plane. Atticus hasn't stopped yammering since you got kidnapped. He's really scared."

"We all are," Dan told her meaningfully. "And with good reason."

"I'm not afraid anymore," his sister said honestly. "Maybe that's just the serum talking — the stuff's awful, but it definitely clears your thinking. The two of us have been squabbling ever since this began, and here's where it ends. Stopping Pierce is too important. When we fight, we weaken ourselves and strengthen the enemy." She held out her hand. "Truce?"

"Truce," Dan agreed, and they shook.

She nearly crushed every bone from the wrist down.

CHAPTER 5

A prison was still a prison, regardless of whether or not your jailers appreciated your baking.

Nellie Gomez stood behind the counter of the commissary of Trilon Labs, Pierce's secret facility in Delaware, her hair stuffed inside a tall chef's hat and latex gloves on her hands. She placed a small dessert dish on the tray of the scientist in front of her.

He regarded it with approval. "Nellie, I'd walk a mile barefoot on broken glass for your tiramisu."

"Bon appétit," she replied brightly. *Keep smiling, kiddo*, she told herself. *Never let them see that you're plotting against them.*

Three days ago, she'd been posing as a researcher in this place to rescue Cahill scientist—and total hottie—Sammy Mourad. Now she was a prisoner here, exposed as an imposter and forced to serve as Sammy's lab assistant, manufacturing serum for J. Rutherford Pierce. It had been sheer luck that the cook had gotten sick, and she had volunteered to take over the kitchen. Once the scientists realized they had a French-trained chef on the premises, the job was hers. She could already feel the letup in the security that had smothered her and Sammy. True, the guards were still there. But the guns were holstered instead of pointed at her temple from point-blank range. Now the weapons hung at the sides of men who were hunched over servings of chocolate soufflé. It was a key difference.

A good soufflé can perform miracles. That was the motto of her cooking mentor in Paris. Nellie had never wanted to believe it more. If a soufflé or a pastry or even a twelve-course dinner could help Amy, Nellie would move heaven and earth to provide it.

Poor Amy, with only a handful of days left to live. Only the antidote could save her, and the ingredients for that lay scattered to the four corners of the globe. Nellie was powerless to aid her kiddo, and the mere thought of that was soul-shattering. Yet it also strengthened her resolve. Maybe she couldn't produce the antidote, but she would do her part in this fight against Pierce. And anyone who got in her way would be flattened.

Another tray slid along the rails, but when Nellie offered a plate, it was rejected. She looked up into Sammy's dark eyes.

"What are you doing, Nellie?" he hissed. "They lock us up like rats, and now you're *cooking* for them?"

"Shhhh," she warned. "The way to people's hearts is through their stomachs."

"Who cares? The squints around here don't call the shots, Pierce does. And he has no heart."

"The more they like my food, the more they'll trust me. And it'll be easier for us to — you know" — she scanned the room, noting the various scientists, their assistants, and the guard du jour, who, although focused on his dessert, never completely took his eyes off her — "sterilize the test tubes."

Sammy nodded. *Sterilize the test tubes* was their private code for their ultimate goal — to destroy the lab. It was bad enough that Pierce had been using the Cahill serum to enhance himself, his rotten kids, and his muscle-headed bodyguards. But as the lab accelerated production of the stuff, he'd soon be able to juice thousands of his goons instead of just dozens. That was the purpose of Trilon — the top secret installation in the basement, anyway — and the reason why Sammy had been kidnapped in the first place.

Lately, though, the scientists had been experimenting with a new formula. The principle involved combining the serum with certain properties of the antidote to create a kind of super-serum. "Franken-serum," Nellie called it. It would be one-dose, extra powerful, and would avoid all the usual side effects. If the Cahills were to have any chance of derailing the Pierce freight train, Nellie and Sammy had to knock out the lab before the Franken-serum became a reality.

"We'll talk later," she hissed, forcing the plate on him.

As Sammy headed for a table, she turned her attention to the next person coming along the line. His name was Dr. Jeffrey Callender, head of the Callender Institute in New York City, where Fiske Cahill was a patient. The elderly Fiske was not doing well, and Dr. Callender was the reason why. His institute was testing the serum on poor Fiske — exposing him to dangerously high doses and monitoring the side effects. Callender was in cahoots with Pierce all the way, and the two of them were using the old man as a lab rat.

"Don't skip dessert, Jeffrey," Callender's lunch partner advised. "Our Nellie is Paris trained."

Dr. Callender peered down his long nose at Nellie. "Miss Gomez and I are already acquainted."

"It's a pleasure to see you again, Doctor," Nellie said sweetly. *It would be an even greater pleasure to take a baseball bat to your lousy head.*

Of course, she couldn't say that aloud. So when no one was looking, Nellie discreetly spit in a dish of tiramisu before placing it on Callender's tray. "Enjoy."

That was something else she'd learned in Paris.

According to the tracking beacon on Pony's computer, the Pierce jet was heading for Siem Reap in Cambodia, the closest airport to the ancient ruins of Angkor.

"It's too dangerous to follow them there," Jake decided. "They'll arrive with just enough time to set up an ambush."

"Let them try," Amy said brashly. "We can take

them."

Their eyes locked. Amy was known for keeping a cool head, but that had changed. Now that she felt she could beat the Pierce goons in a fair fight, she seemed to be spoiling for one.

The two turned to Dan, who looked up in surprise.

Like it or not, it was his job to make a call on their next move. "Let's try to avoid a smackdown until we have the antidote. Maybe we can fly into a different airport and make it to Angkor without Pierce's goons noticing."

"There's something I don't quite understand," Ian ventured. "How was Pony tracking Pierce's plane? He couldn't have infiltrated the crew and planted a transmitter on board. He was a hacker, not a secret agent."

"Maybe he wasn't tracking the plane at all," Atticus suggested. "What if he was tracking somebody *on* it?"

"However he did it," Dan said mournfully, "it wasn't worth the price he paid."

Amy was dabbing cream on Dan's scorched cheek with her left hand, which was less susceptible to her tremors. She paused, and their unspoken grief and regret bubbled up to fill the silence. Pony had joined them willingly. But there was no denying that the gutsy digital cowboy would be alive today if he'd never crossed paths with Amy and Dan.

"We should get some sleep," she said quickly. "We've got four hours before we land, and I doubt it's going to be very relaxing after that."

Phnom Penh was Cambodia's capital, and **h**ome to the largest airport in the country. Jonah was held up in Passport Control **b**ecause the customs agents all wanted autog**ra**phs. But the star was eve**n**tually able to **c**onvince **h**is fans that h**e** was**n**'t pl**a**nning any Cambodian conce**r**t dat**e**s or pu**b**lic **a**ppearan**c**es.

"I'm just a tourist, yo, chec**k**ing out your country's slamming sights," he assured them.

At last, with their famous cousin properly hidden behind sunglasses and a baseball cap, the Cahill party emerged from the baggage claim.

"Guys!" came a familiar voice. "Over here!" It was muscle-bound Hamilton Holt, a head taller and at least sixty pounds heavier than everybody else at the airport.

"My man!" Jonah reached his cousin first, and the two shared a vigorous embrace that looked more like a wrestling match. They were unlikely best friends — the brawny Tomas and the flashy, artsy Janus — but each would have walked through walls for the other.

"We'll need an SUV to fit all seven of us," Amy decided.

"Not necessary," Hamilton informed her. "I got us a boat."

"Why?" Ian was flabbergasted. "We're two hundred miles from Angkor!"

"It's just as fast," Hamilton promised. "And it'll be good to have it once we get there. We're looking for the Tonle Sap water snake. Guess which river goes all the way from here to Angkor—the Tonle Sap! I picked up some fishing nets. Maybe we'll get lucky and nab a snake on the trip."

"Except that they're practically extinct!" Ian pointed out.

"Really?" Hamilton was floored. "How are we supposed to catch one?"

"Welcome to the world of the Cahills," Dan sighed in an exhausted tone. "If it isn't impossible, it isn't worth doing."

Their boat was listed as a "luxury craft," which meant it had a canvas sun shield nailed to a rotting frame. Its name was the *Kaoh Kong*, which Dan and Atticus immediately dubbed the *King Kong*.

Phnom Penh was located at the intersection of the Tonle Sap and Mekong Rivers. "The boat rental guy drew me a map," Hamilton explained as the motor roared to life in a cloud of blue oil smoke. "It's a no-brainer. You head north and hang a left at the fork. After that, it's a straight shot to Siem Reap and Angkor. What could go wrong?"

What went wrong was something the "boat rental guy" hadn't bothered to mention. The Tonle Sap River was a torrent during the monsoon rains. But this was dry season, when the mighty waterway shriveled to a muddy creek. Even at maximum speed, the trip would take at least eight grueling hours in breathless heat and humidity.

In order to pass the time productively, they took turns casting two nets over the side in the hope that they might snare a water snake. All they caught, however, were a handful of catfish, and a few dead birds.

Jonah lay beneath the canopy, his arms and legs spread in an attempt to attract what little breeze there was. "I'm not asking for the *Queen Mary*, but this is medieval."

"London never gets this hot," moaned Ian. "At least, not since the great fire of 1666."

"Forget the heat." Jake was beside himself. "We're wasting *eight hours* of Amy's life! Surely even the bus would be faster than this!"

Amy cast a jaundiced eye in his direction. She understood his anguish—he was a powerless spectator as the effects of the serum ravaged her. Still, she needed him to stop trying to protect her. "It's better this way," she said stoutly. "Airports and bus stations can be watched, but no one will be expecting us to come crawling up out of the swamp."

From his place behind the wheel, Hamilton looked grateful for her support. He knew he was being blamed for the general discomfort.

Amy was putting a brave face on it, but she was suffering more than anybody. The arm and leg tremors were becoming harder and harder to hide. Scarier still, the jungle heat seemed to accelerate her hallucinations. At one point, she flattened herself to the deck to avoid a diving tropical bird that wasn't there. How could she explain *that* to Jake and Dan, who both rarely took their eyes off her?

They were too hot to enjoy the sights — picturesque fishing villages of ingeniously devised bamboo dwellings along the river. Heavy sedimentation gave the water a texture that resembled woven fabric, stretched out for miles before their craft. Giant catfish broke the surface before disappearing again. Water buffalo watched them pass with calm interest, lowing among themselves as if discussing the strange newcomers.

"No autographs, yo," Jonah mumbled at them in a sleepy haze.

Atticus, the linguistic genius, had a working knowledge of Khmer. But it turned out to be *ancient* Khmer, so all he got from the fishermen they encountered were blank stares. Jake tried calling out the word for *snake* and waving fistfuls of US dollars and Cambodian riels. The locals looked like they wanted to take the money, but they couldn't supply the snakes.

Beyond the village of Kampong Chhnang, the waterway became wider and deeper, and they were able to increase speed. After six hours of near-total sameness, the scenery began to change dramatically. The river widened into a vast lake, glassy calm, rimmed with fishing communities built out into the water on the narrowest of land spits.

"This is the Tonle Sap," Atticus explained. "It really is a Great Lake!"

"It's beautiful!" Amy exclaimed. They seemed to be sailing into a gigantic liquid mirror, with the clouds and sky perfectly replicated across the placid surface. "And to think that half the country depends on this fishing ground for most of its protein."

They made great time crossing the broad expanse of the lake before slowing down again to navigate the Siem Reap River, a narrow tributary that led to their destination. Once again, they were crawling along a narrow stream surrounded by jungle.

They passed a few more ramshackle dwellings, and then Jonah pointed. "Check it out — the houses around here are all made of Popsicle sticks. So how come that one up ahead looks like Malibu?"

They all craned their necks to stare. Around the bend was a California-esque luxury home. Beyond that was one built in the Mississippi River style. All variety of boats were tied up at docks along the waterfront — not just homemade fishing dugouts, but imported pleasure craft.

"Suburbs," Jake concluded. "That means we're close to a city."

Soon the thick jungle growth gave way to landscaping, and the buildings of Siem Reap came into view. It was not a large metropolis with skyscrapers and the smokestacks of heavy industry. But compared with the primitive villages they had passed on the river, it was modern and inviting.

There was no formal marina, so Hamilton skillfully moored the *Kaoh Kong* to a piling beside several other boats.

"Solid ground," Ian said worshipfully as he stepped off the dock onto the grassy riverbank. "I never thought I'd stand on it again."

Jonah was equally appreciative. "Air-conditioning! Showers! I've got monster stage sweat without the stage!"

"If you don't like my rent-a-boat, next time you can swim along beside it," Hamilton commented, his beefy arms akimbo. "I'm sure the catfish will appreciate the company."

Dan took charge. "Siem Reap is the closest city to Angkor, so a lot of tourists come here. Let's pick the best hotel in town and book a whole floor of suites!"

"That's not how you keep a low profile," Amy lectured. "We want a place where Galt would never look for us."

"Understood," Ian acknowledged. "In the interest of safety, we must accept four stars instead of five."

"How about *no* stars," Amy suggested. "A guesthouse run by an old lady who doesn't talk about her guests."

"Fine," sighed Ian. "So long as it provides plush bathrobes and fuzzy slippers."

Jake laughed in his face. "Brace yourself, Kabra. Get ready to see how the other half lives."

CHAPTER 6

The hotel was called Jayavarman — Sleep Here, named for a famous line of ancient Khmer kings. There were no plush bathrobes and fuzzy slippers, and no need for them. There was also no pool and no air-conditioning, so it was far too hot for extra clothing.

Atticus described it as "a bed and breakfast minus the breakfast and minus the beds." They slept on rush mats on the bamboo floor. Every time somebody rolled over, the sound was like a vast army of ants marching in unison. There was little furniture and no TV.

But it was clean, spacious, and relatively bug-free, thanks to the mosquito netting just about everywhere. Better still, the owner, Mrs. Bopha, spoke no language known to humankind or even to Atticus. She couldn't betray the Cahills' location even if Galt Pierce found her and interrogated her personally.

"It's perfect," declared Amy. "The whole world thinks we're spoiled rich kids. This is the last place anyone would look for us."

"Nobody would look for us in the sewer, either," Dan

pointed out sourly. "That doesn't mean we should start hanging out there."

"Look at this." Ian sat cross-legged on his sleeping mat, peering at the computer in perplexity. "Whatever Pony was tracking, it's here in Siem Reap." He turned the screen around so they could clearly see the pulsating beacon moving through the streets.

"That's not too far from here," Dan observed. "Maybe we should check it out."

"Not so fast," Jake jumped in. "What if it's Galt and Cara?"

The door burst open and in staggered Hamilton and Jonah, dripping wet in their bathing suits, snapping towels at each other, sending a spray all around the room.

Ian slammed the laptop shut. "Savages! If we ruin this computer, then where will we be? Up the Tonle Sap without a paddle, that's where!"

"That shower is awesome, yo!" Jonah cackled.

"It's an outdoor stall with a bucket of water on a swivel," Hamilton hiccupped. "When you pull the rope, it dumps all over you!"

"I was thinking of putting in a wave pool at my crib in LA," Jonah added. "But maybe I'll just get one of these. I'll save a fortune! Remind me to text a picture to my architect."

Dan and Atticus exchanged a meaningful glance. Instantly, they were digging swimsuits out of their backpacks and sprinting for the door.

"Should we stop them?" Jake asked Amy. "We really need to get to work."

"Let them have some fun," Amy said with a sad smile. "The trouble with the whole Cahill thing is that it steals your childhood."

And some of us might not stay alive long enough to become adults.

Twenty-seven miles east of the rockbound coast of Maine, a true jewel of New England rose from the waves. Originally known as Shattuck's Folly, the island had been renamed Pierce Landing by the new owner, J. Rutherford Pierce. He'd wanted to call it Pierceland, but his political team had advised against it. It would appear un-American, they said, to set up what sounded like a private country right on the doorstep of the United States.

Of course, if Rutherford has his way, the entire USA and the rest of the world, too, will be Pierceland soon enough, reflected Debi Ann Pierce as the cameras from *60 Minutes* rolled.

Rutherford revealed none of this to the reporter, of course. Technically, he wasn't even a candidate for president yet.

"Well, Steve," he said smoothly, "I'm not ready to talk about my future at the moment. But the whole country is invited to Pierce Landing on May fifth for my All-American Clambake. That's when I'll be unveiling my plans." He chuckled. "I wish I could host every single citizen right here on the island. But that would be a tight squeeze, even for this big old place. So I urge everybody to watch us on TV. We're going to be doing great things together, America and I, because this land is *our* land. . . ."

Well behind the cameras, in a small sitting area, Debi Ann sewed a button nose on one of her hand-crafted teddy bears. *Another interview*, she thought with a sigh. It was up to three a day now. She could only imagine how many there would be after her husband's big announcement. Once he was officially the Patriotist candidate for president, his schedule would become even more frenetic, and he would have no time at all for her and the kids. She had to accept this as the fate of the wife of a great statesman.

She snipped the last thread, stuck the needle in her pincushion, and sat back to admire her handiwork. There was a timeless quality to her teddy bears. They differed very little from the very first ones, created during the time of Teddy Roosevelt. It was thrilling to consider that she and her family might soon be living in the same White House once home to the great man himself.

She got up to find a place for the new bear in her breakfront cabinet. She frowned. It was quite full already. Rutherford was so busy, and Galt and Cara had been traveling as well. That had left Debi Ann alone a lot — and her teddy bear production had increased.

As she began to shift her creations to free up space, a leather-bound book slipped out from behind a black bear and fell to the floor at her feet.

What was this? She picked it up, noting its yellowed pages and musty smell. The inside cover read:

> *Olivia Behan Cahill*
> *Household Book*
> *Anno Domini 1499*

Olivia Cahill! Debi Ann experienced a shiver of excitement at the enormity of this discovery. Olivia was the matriarch of the entire Cahill family! Wife of Gideon! Mother of Luke, Katherine, Thomas, Jane, and Madeleine!

Debi Ann's family — the Starlings — were part of the brilliant Ekaterina branch, descended from Katherine. How had this treasure of Cahill history come to be in *her* cabinet, hidden among her bears? Only one person could have put it there — Rutherford. He wasn't a Cahill. Why would he have such an item?

She began to flip through the brittle pages, unable to make sense of more than a word or two. There were Post-it notes here and there, and those certainly hadn't come from 1499. They were mostly questions, written in Rutherford's unmistakable bold hand: *Take to cryptographer . . . Meaning behind poem? . . . Double-check locations . . .*

And the one that made her heart beat a little faster: *Connection to Hope?*

Hope Cahill, daughter of the legendary Grace. The next thought made her flinch, even after all these years. Rutherford had been madly in love with Hope Cahill. He had pursued her with the same fanatical singleness of purpose with which he pursued everything else — including the presidency. Debi Ann knew she'd been second choice, and her husband had only turned to her after Hope had married Arthur Trent. If Rutherford couldn't have the Cahill he wanted, then he'd take the Cahill who was available.

Tears stung her eyes. After all these years and two beautiful children — and with Hope long gone — nothing had changed. When Rutherford had found this Cahill heirloom, his first thought had been not of his own wife, but of Hope.

She was competing with a dead woman. And losing.

Rutherford had always been ambitious, but ever since the presidency had appeared on his radar screen, his obsession with achieving his goals had swelled to the point where there was no room for anything else in his life.

Debi Ann had once believed that his wife and children were immune to this, that they would always retain a special place in Rutherford's heart. Now she suspected they were just three more pawns on the vast, complex chessboard of his Grand Plan.

Pawns that could be sacrificed.

CHAPTER 7

The *Kaoh Kong* bobbed by the pylon in the Siem Reap River, exactly where they'd left it.

Dan was amazed. "The *King Kong* is still here. I love this town! People are so trustworthy. Look, nobody even stole our fishing nets!"

That day, the search began in earnest for the final antidote ingredient. Amy, Dan, Jake, and Atticus drew snake-fishing duty, while Hamilton and Jonah went off to investigate one of the local crocodile farms. The Tonle Sap water snake had once been the most popular crocodile food in Cambodia. Maybe their quarry was still being used as feed—at least unofficially.

Only Ian was excused from the snake hunt. According to the beacon on the Ponyrific computer, whoever the digital cowboy had been tracking was somewhere in the Angkor region, possibly in pursuit of the very same antidote component. It was Ian's job to identify exactly who this potential competitor might be.

The winding Siem Reap River took the *Kaoh Kong* north and east toward the ruins of Angkor, just a few miles beyond the city.

"In actuality," Atticus lectured as Jake maneuvered the boat away from the shore, "Angkor was not a single city. Each Khmer king built his own capital somewhere in the area, so it's all pretty spread out."

Amy was examining a tourist map. "It looks like all these sites are temples. Where did the people live?"

When it came to lost civilizations, Atticus Rosenbloom was never stumped. "All homes, from the lowliest hut to the king's palace, were built of wood. The only buildings considered important enough to be made out of stone were temples. So they're the ones that survived."

"Like the Three Little Pigs," Dan added wisely. "The straw house and the stick house blew away. But when the big bad wolf came to the brick house —"

"Did the three little pigs ever build anything like *that*?" Jake interrupted, pointing upriver.

They all turned to stare. Out of the jungle rose five stunning stone towers.

"Angkor Wat," Atticus breathed reverently.

"Angkor *what*?" echoed Dan.

Atticus giggled. For a genius who had finished high school in his "spare time" at age eleven, he had a kindergarten sense of humor.

"Captain — weigh Angkor!" Dan added.

Amy shot them an exasperated expression. "Cut it out, you guys."

"Don't get mad," her brother returned. "Where's

your Angkor management?"

Amy's eyes met Jake's, and the older teenagers laughed in spite of their dire situation. Atticus was a bona fide genius, and Dan was the leader of the most powerful family in human history, but the two of them could be such a pair of knuckleheads sometimes.

Amy had almost forgotten Jake's infectious grin, which made his amazing eyes appear even greener.

Atticus's smiled turned to a look of wonder as he returned his attention to the famed, soaring silhouettes. "Angkor Wat is the largest religious monument in the world," Atticus was explaining to Dan.

Dan peered at the distant towers. "Which one is it?"

"All of them," Atticus supplied.

And then Dan saw. What had appeared to be several separate structures turned out to be one enormous whole. The gray sandstone seemed to shimmer in the bright sunlight, giving the vast temple an otherworldly appearance. The word *imposing* didn't even come close—especially when he realized that the tiny dots moving on the multitiered galleries were tourists.

"We aren't even close enough to appreciate how big it really is," Amy announced in a hushed tone.

"The towers are designed in the style of lotus blossoms," Atticus continued. "It's a major theme in Khmer architecture. Although most temples face east, Angkor Wat faces west. That could be because it's also a funerary monument."

As the *Kaoh Kong* took them upriver, the lotus towers

of Angkor Wat seemed to soar into the sky, the central spire reaching a height well over two hundred feet. At one point, through a clearing in the tree cover, they could see the outer wall and even catch a glimpse of sparkling water.

Dan was confused. "Is it on an island?"

"That's the moat," Atticus explained. "The ancient Angkorians were masters at dredging waterways. A lot of the major temples have them."

They had not fully passed Angkor Wat when other, smaller temples began to rise out of the jungle, providing a sense of the size and complexity of the great civilization that had once existed here.

"Okay, I get it," Dan said finally. "Anybody who could build all this would have been smart enough to have big-time knowledge to pass on. It makes sense that a key ingredient could come from here."

Amy pulled up the fishing nets and removed several twigs and a Coke can with the logo written in Khmer. "The ancient Angkorians had something we don't — a whole river full of Tonle Sap water snakes."

As she spoke, the tallest tower of Angkor Wat morphed into a gigantic serpent and hissed at her, forked tongue waving.

Part of her understood it was only a hallucination. But she ducked anyway.

CHAPTER 8

The Rith Map Crocodile Farm was located halfway between Siem Reap and Tonle Sap Lake. It was a ten-minute drive by *tuk-tuk*, the three-wheeled motorized rickshaw taxis popular in town. That included a short side trip to drop off a 106-year-old woman, whose live chicken kept pecking Hamilton's muscular arm.

At last they reached Rith Map, which translated to "strong and fat," apparently desirable qualities in a crocodile. The tourists certainly seemed to think so—the place was packed, and Hamilton and Jonah had to stand in line for nearly an hour outside the ramshackle hut that served as Rith Map's box office.

"Keep a low profile," Hamilton muttered to his cousin, who was hidden behind sunglasses beneath the brim of his Dodgers cap. "This place is full of Western tourists. If you get recognized, they'll tear you to pieces faster than the crocodiles ever could."

"Word," Jonah acknowledged, pulling the hat down lower over his famous features.

Finally, they bought their tickets and made it onto

the property. The "farm" was a series of muddy pits and swampy ponds, filled with crocodiles of all sizes, ranging from animals a few feet long to several monsters that might have measured almost twenty, including their massive muscular tails.

"Hard to believe I sicced one of these monsters on Amy and Dan in Egypt," Jonah commented, surveying the expanse of powerful jaws and sharp teeth. "You know, back when we were all at each other's throats, looking for the clues. What a difference a couple of years makes."

"The Tomas used to offer alligator wrestling at summer camp," Hamilton told him. "I never signed up, though. Dodgeball was my game. Three-time champion."

A crowded terrace overlooked the property, but the more intrepid visitors were able to go down a rickety staircase to a path that wound among the habitats via a series of footbridges. As Jonah and Hamilton started down, attendants in khakis appeared on the bridges. An announcement was made in Khmer, followed by the English translation:

"Feeding time!"

The attendants began to toss fish and raw meat into the pens. The response from the crocs was colossal. Normally slow and ponderous, they darted after the food, churning the water into a spray and fighting one another for every morsel. The cacophony of snapping jaws, colliding bodies, and splashing water was like a kindergarten rhythm band, blood-sport edition. Three feet in front of Hamilton and Jonah, a ham hock, bone in, disappeared down a massive gullet like it was a bonbon.

It ended as suddenly as it had begun. With almost a single mind, the crocs seemed to decide that there was no more lunch coming, so why bother expending energy trying to kill each other to get to it? They settled back into their languid poses in and around the water, and it was as if the frenzy had never taken place. Of all the hundreds of pounds of food that had been thrown into the enclosures, not a scrap remained.

With effort, Jonah tore his attention from the spectacle they had just witnessed to the purpose of their visit to Rith Map. "That was some tight smorgasbord," he said with respect. "But I got to say I saw a lot of chow go down the hatch—fish, meat, small animals, and birds. The one thing I didn't see—"

"Snakes," Hamilton finished in a somber tone. "And they're supposed to be the number one croc food." He approached the nearest attendant. "Nice show, buddy. Hamilton Holt from the United States. Do you speak English?"

The man nodded. "Also French, German, Japanese, little Italian. People come to Angkor from everywhere."

"Word," Jonah acknowledged. "Slamming snappers, yo."

The attendant looked blank. "That language I not know."

"I heard that the best food for these guys is the Tonle Sap water snake," Hamilton went on. "How come you didn't feed them any of that?"

"Not enough snakes anymore," the man replied seriously. "Crocs need much food. You see this."

"Come on, the snakes can't be *that* rare," Hamilton coaxed. "We're ready to pay good money for one. US dollars. Name your price."

The man was outraged. "Not allowed. Snake protected by government!"

Jonah's sharp eyes had been watching the smaller satellite pond to their left. Something was swimming down there, its long, thin body moving in an undulating wave as it kept its distance from the crocodiles. "Yo, there's a snake. Isn't that the right kind?"

"You may not touch! Threatened species!"

"We're not going to whack him," Jonah wheedled. "We just need some venom! We'll let him go!"

"You must ask permission!" insisted the attendant.

"No time!" roared Hamilton. In an instant, he vaulted over the rail and landed with a titanic splash in the satellite pond.

The sight of him in the aquatic habitat of carnivorous reptiles was enough to shatter even Jonah's legendary cool. *"Yo!"* he shouted. *"What's up with you, man?"*

But Hamilton was already stroking across the muddy water in a textbook freestyle. Oblivious to his pursuit, the little snake continued to flutter around. There was only a handful of crocodiles in the satellite pond, and they barely reacted at all. They watched with lifeless, almost bored expressions, as if the presence of a big linebacker kicking up a spray like a cabin cruiser was an everyday occurrence.

Hamilton's arms worked like the blades of a windmill, drawing him ever closer to the source of the final ingredient. Then, with his reaching hand just a few inches shy of its quarry, a large mouth broke the surface, yawned open around the snake, and snapped shut.

Fearless, Hamilton grasped the long, dangerous snout and tried to pry it open. "Don't even think about swallowing, you walking suitcase!"

The struggle was on. Hamilton pulled with all the strength of his ancestors, but he could not budge those massive jaws. "Come on, cough it up!"

He paid no attention to the screams coming from the spectators, the loudest of these from his own cousin: "Get out of there, you dumb Tomas, before you get your buzz cut bitten off!"

Hamilton did not see what Jonah and the other visitors did — that three more crocs were converging on the site of the disturbance, skimming silently across the water.

Without another thought — because if he'd had a thought, he never would have done it — Jonah leaped over the side and into the habitat. As he broke the surface, his glasses fell off and his hat went sailing through the air, only to be snapped up by an enormous set of jaws.

The shrieks grew even louder.

"It's Jonah Wizard!"

"He's trying to rescue that big guy!"

"Save Jonah Wizard!"

At that moment, the trained staff of the farm stampeded into the pond, wielding long wooden sticks to keep the crocodiles at bay.

"Out of water!" commanded the English-speaking attendant.

"Not without my snake!" Hamilton replied in a strained voice.

"It's not your snake!" Jonah indicated the struggling croc in Hamilton's grip. "It's *his* snake now! Give it up, and let's bounce!"

"Fine," Hamilton agreed sulkily. "So how do you let go?"

"How should I know?" Jonah was close to hysterical. "You're the one who went to Tomas camp!"

"I told you — I took dodgeball!"

Another attendant came over and cinched a cord around the crocodile's long snout.

"Out of water," repeated the English-speaking man. "Leave Rith Map. Never return."

Jonah was mobbed by fans as the two climbed onto the footbridge. Cameras and phones flashed.

"Thanks," Jonah greeted his public. "'Preciate the love." He gave a slight wave, swayed once, and passed out cold into Hamilton's arms.

CHAPTER 9

"The interior is decorated by more than one thousand, eight hundred *apsaras* — celestial nymphs," announced the tour guide. "According to myth, they were born from the Churning of the Ocean of Milk."

Most Londoners believed their city was the greatest cultural capital of the world. But even Ian had to admit there was nothing in London the size and scale of Angkor Wat. Who built a room large enough for eighteen hundred bas-relief statues? True, the original works by Rodin in the sculpture garden of the Kabra mansion were nearly as fine — if not as numerous. That, of course, was Rodin's failing, not Vikram Kabra's. If Rodin had created eighteen hundred statues, Ian was sure his father would have spared no expense collecting them all.

The thought of Vikram Kabra brought out a stab of longing. Father, living in estrangement somewhere in South America; Mother and Natalie gone. When Ian had first met Amy and Dan, he'd called them pathetic orphans. The memory of the cruel jab made his face hot with shame.

He returned his attention to the magnificence around him. King Suryavarman II, who built this place in the early twelfth century, must have been a bigger-is-better kind of fellow. And if his goal had been to impress people, he'd succeeded beyond his wildest dreams. *Too well*, Ian thought in annoyance. It was almost impossible to get a steady Wi-Fi signal in this massive stone complex. Their guide already hated Ian for keeping one eye on Pony's laptop. He had even said, "Your full attention, if you please!" a couple of times.

Like I'm playing video games, not trying to save the world, Ian thought resentfully.

And now that the Internet kept dropping out every few minutes, he had to devote even more of his concentration to the computer. The guide was forgetting his speech, and the other tourists were blaming Ian.

An ugly scene in Angkor Wat certainly wouldn't help the Cahills' efforts to keep a low profile.

But how could he ignore what he was seeing on the screen? According to Pony's tracking program, the pulsing red dot was very close. On top of him, practically — inside Angkor Wat's moat!

I have to get higher up, he decided. *And outside.*

To the guide's immense relief, Ian slipped away from the group in search of a staircase. In ancient times, only the king and the high priest were allowed on the top level, but Wi-Fi hadn't been a concern in those days. This was a necessity.

The climb wasn't easy—forty steps pitched at a steep angle. At the apex, he found himself breathless, and a little bit dizzy. The five immense lotus towers loomed over the entire structure from this level, blocking out the sun. But reception was perfect. The beacon pulsed clear and true, directly below him.

He rushed to the outer gallery and peered over the side. The view was spectacular—the western causeway crossing the moat, the surrounding landscape, dotted with glistening reservoirs and smaller temples. Ian barely saw any of it. For at the base of the structure far below sat a blond girl, her fingers dancing on the keyboard of a laptop that sat on a stone parapet in front of her. She glanced up for a moment, and even at this distance, Ian was struck by the notion that he should recognize her. . . .

In the airy tranquility of Angkor Wat's highest level, the harsh beep from Pony's computer might as well have been a bomb blast. Startled, Ian looked at the screen. An angry pop-up declared: *OUTSIDE ACCESS DENIED*. Another beep: *OUTSIDE ACCESS DENIED*. What was going on? Ian traced his finger on the track pad, but the computer had locked up, stuck in an endless loop of warning sounds and messages. This went on until the machine emitted a softer, more welcoming tone, and a new message appeared: *ACCESS GRANTED*.

The frozen monitor came back to life. Ian watched in horror as columns of documents began to disappear. Someone was wiping Pony's hard drive!

The greatest hacker in the world had been hacked!

The familiar blond girl pounding her keyboard. It couldn't be a coincidence — *she* was doing this!

According to Pony, there was only one person whose skills rivaled his own — Pierce's hacker, April May.

Ian peered down at her. Could *this* be the ruthless and mysterious April May? A teenage girl? A hacker could be anybody, anywhere — a ninety-year-old great-grandmother in Vladivostock, a disgruntled troublemaker on an oil rig in the North Sea, even an astronaut aboard the International Space Station.

Yet the more Ian mulled it over, the more it made perfect sense for April May to be a kid. Pony himself hadn't been much older than this girl. After all, hacking was a young person's game. Most older adults had too much trouble with the technology.

He recalled the computer's initial alert that the tracking program had picked up a signal: *Code A*. It had to be! Pony had been tracking his greatest rival, who was working for Pierce! And it also explained why April May had abandoned her secure remote location to travel to Cambodia. She had discovered that her defenses had been penetrated and had gone off in search of the computer that had done the job.

None of this helps save Pony's computer, Ian thought in a panic, watching the precious files wink out of existence like glowing embers in the wind.

He threw the laptop under his arm and ran for the stairs, sidestepping down the steep flight to avoid overbalancing himself and taking a swan dive into the stone floor below. At the second level, he became entangled in his former tour group, and had to shove his way through to the next set of steps.

"You Americans and your electronic toys!" the guide muttered under his breath.

Such was Ian's haste to reach the ultimate hacker that he dared not take the few extra seconds required to point out that he was, in fact, British. He blasted down the longer staircase to ground level, fully expecting her to be gone. But there she was, still at her keyboard, looking relaxed and comfortable, as if she *hadn't* just made mincemeat of the only hacker who had ever been able to stand up to her.

Ian stopped short, amazed. No wonder she had seemed familiar. He *knew* her. They had met just weeks ago in Ireland. She'd been a redhead then, but there was no mistaking her heart-shaped face and luminous eyes. She had tricked him that time—totally bamboozled would have been a better way to describe it. He set his jaw. It would not happen again.

"April May!" he snapped accusingly.

"Ian Kabra," she acknowledged. There was no sign of her Irish brogue. The accent was American. "We meet again. You're kind of cute when you're mad."

"Then I must be one of those kittens on YouTube you Americans are so fond of turning into viral video stars! What are you doing to my computer? And why?"

"I don't like people tracking me."

"If you're April May, you know perfectly well it wasn't me. It was Pony. And he won't track you anymore because he's dead. Dropped out of a helicopter. By the people you work for. You must be proud."

Ian expected her to laugh in his face. Or at least roll her eyes. So he was surprised when she flinched and looked away. "I don't work for them. I *am* them."

"If you think you can fool me again—"

She looked genuinely incredulous. "You don't recognize me?"

His initial reaction—as any Lucian's would be—was suspicion. But a closer inspection of the girl brought about an astonishing revelation. The blond hair, the fair features, the palpable vitality. She was a *Pierce*!

How could he have missed it? J. Rutherford Pierce was more famous than Jonah Wizard these days. "Cara Pierce?" he blurted.

She nodded.

Ian's head was spinning. "But why the secret identity? We all know April May works for Pierce. Why keep it a mystery that you're his daughter?"

"You don't get it." She shook her head. "I'm not hiding the truth from *you*; I'm hiding it from *him*. He has no idea that I'm April May!"

Ian was flabbergasted. "Why would you keep that from your own father?"

She stared at him for a long moment. When she spoke at last, there was an edge in her voice. "You have no idea what it's like when you can't trust your own parent."

He was so startled that he retreated a half step. The truth was that Ian knew *exactly* what it was like. He almost told her so, but this wasn't the time and place. Those were memories he'd forced into the deepest recesses of his mind but that still kept him awake at night. Ian's father had literally dropped off the grid in an attempt to escape the disgrace of his wife's legacy. Ian's sister, Natalie, hadn't been so lucky. She had died trying to stop their mother.

"Still," Ian said aloud, "there's a big difference between not trusting your father and actively deceiving him." Growing up as the first son of the Lucian leadership, Ian had been taught that deceit was pointless in the absence of an underlying strategy. "What's your angle?"

"Well, first off, the money's good," she replied. "A high-end cowboy doesn't come cheap."

"Cowboy," Ian echoed wanly. Pony used to refer to himself that way.

"But to be totally honest" — she looked around furtively — "I'm afraid of him. He has plans — terrible plans —"

"What plans?"

She blinked, her eyes closing an instant longer than necessary. "All I can say is that the presidency is just the beginning. As his daughter, I'd never be able to stop him. As his hacker, on the other hand —"

"That still wouldn't give you the power to shut him down," Ian insisted.

"No," she agreed sadly. "But at least now I can keep an eye on his activities."

Ian was skeptical. "And you expect me to believe all that."

"I can help you find the antidote," she ventured suddenly.

"Why would you want to help us?"

"Because even though I hate what my father's trying to do, I still love *him*. The serum is killing him. It's probably killing me, too. My dad tries to hide his tremors, but we all know they're getting worse."

Ian knew the debilitating effects of the serum as well as anybody. He had to look no farther than his own mother's horrible death and Amy's worsening condition to see Gideon's creation in action. Still, he offered no reaction that might reveal to Cara that she was beginning to make sense to him. That wasn't the Lucian way.

Apparently, she interpreted his silence as skepticism. "You think it's easy to reach out to people my father considers the enemy? I don't mean to stab him in the back, but I'm desperate!"

"You *are* stabbing him in the back," Ian pointed out. "At least, he'll see it that way."

"I don't care," she returned stoutly. "Not if it's the only way to save his life — and maybe a lot of other lives, too. I *need* you guys! We can stop this, but we have to work together."

Ian's mind was awhirl, weighing the pros and cons.

Attractive as she was, this girl was a Pierce, and there-fore not to be believed. She was a notorious hacker who had already duped him in Ireland and—not five min-utes ago—had attacked his computer.

On the other hand, Dan was absolutely convinced that Cara had helped him escape from Pierce's plane on Midway Atoll. That seemed to reinforce an observa-tion Pony had made—that April May's actions hadn't always been 100 percent in support of her boss's goals.

Then again, those things might have been a ruse to make us trust her. . . .

It was a big risk. If they teamed up with Cara, they'd be revealing all the progress they'd made toward the antidote. Yet, now that the enemy had Olivia's book, most of their head start was gone anyway.

With Pierce's advantage in manpower and resources, the Cahills didn't stand a chance. Unless they had a secret weapon—like a double agent inside Pierce's innermost circle.

Now here was Cara, volunteering to be that secret weapon.

As if sensing that he was coming around to her way of thinking, she sweetened the pot. "Here—" She began to work the keyboard of her own computer. "I'll restore Pony's laptop. That was amazing the way he hacked past my defenses. He must have had A-list skills."

"Must have had," Ian repeated numbly, noting the past tense. He opened the machine to see the vanished files reappearing at light speed, sorting themselves into long columns on the screen. Cara also had "A-list skills." And she was offering them to the Cahill cause. . . .

Maybe . . .

Ian wanted so much to believe her. The look in her eyes was achingly familiar.

She's changing sides. Not next week or someday, but right now, standing in front of me.

Ian well remembered the time he'd been forced to make the same agonizing choice — when he'd realized his mother was irredeemably evil, and he had no option but to throw his lot in with Amy and Dan. He could see that shattered loyalty in Cara, feel her guilt and pain. In that way, the daughter of J. Rutherford Pierce was practically his soul mate.

Still, this call was not Ian's to make. Lucians no longer had great influence in the Cahill family, and to his surprise, he wasn't sure that was a bad thing. No, the decision had to come from Amy and Dan. They were in charge.

He turned back to Cara. "We'll let you know."

She nodded. "I'll text you my secure contact info. I have your number."

That was something Ian knew well. Back in Ireland, she'd put a tracker on his phone. It had almost gotten them all killed.

He smiled.

It took a special girl to make Ian Kabra fear for his life.

CHAPTER 10

In the stern of the *Kaoh Kong*, Dan and Atticus had their shirts off and were splashing themselves with river water. It brought no relief from the searing Cambodian heat.

"This is definitely worse than Guatemala," Dan griped. "I mean, the *humidity*! It's like you're carrying a ton of wet laundry on your shoulders."

"In actuality—" Atticus began.

Dan cut him off. "Yeah, I get it. It's impossible to carry a ton of laundry."

"I was just going to say that even my dreadlocks are sweating," Atticus explained. "They're great for Boston winters. Here—not so much."

"Stop complaining and check the nets again," ordered Jake from behind the wheel.

"We checked three minutes ago," his brother whined.

"In those three minutes, we might have caught a snake."

"Fat chance of that," Dan mourned. "In the old

days, you'd stick your foot in the river, and there'd be a Tonle Sap water snake hanging off of each toe. Now they're all gone. Just our luck!"

"It wasn't very lucky for the snakes, either," Atticus noted.

Amy was stretched across a row of life preservers in the bow. She was having trouble distinguishing between the heat shimmer in the air and her personal hallucinatory light show. She saw monkeys in every tree, which was confusing, because she knew for a fact that there were *some* monkeys in *some* trees. But she also knew there was no monkey on Jake's shoulder. Yet there it was, leering at her.

There were voices, too—voices from the past that she understood could not possibly be real—her parents, Grace, Uncle Alistair. There was even an old man she somehow knew to be Gideon Cahill: "Why would you take that potion, child?"

She looked astern, only to see Pony seated between Dan and Atticus, being drenched by their water fight. And beyond them, a shiny speedboat coming up fast in the river traffic.

Amy squinted in the relentless sun. Galt Pierce was standing in the bow. *Why can't he be a hallucination?*

But Galt was all too real, and so were the five muscle-heads with him.

She pointed. "Dan—"

Dan saw them, too. "Goons!" he rasped. "And they're gaining on us!"

Jake pushed forward on the throttle.

"We're going to have to face them sooner or later!" Amy growled. "Now's as good a time as any!"

"That's the serum talking," Jake reasoned as the *Kaoh Kong* sped up and began to pass slower craft.

"Maybe the serum's right this time," Amy argued. "Let me bust some heads with it before it kills me!"

"Those guys may not be as juiced as you, but there are six of them!" Dan pointed out. "And the rest of us aren't juiced at all!"

Amy's faith in her physical abilities trumped all logic. "Turn the boat around! We'll ram them!"

"Nobody's ramming anybody!" Jake shouted.

"In actuality," Atticus said in a high-pitched tone, "I think *we're* the ones about to get rammed!"

The speedboat was fairly flying now, weaving around the slow-moving mail packets and tourist craft.

"Not if I have anything to say about it!" Jake put his full weight into the throttle, and the *Kaoh Kong* surged ahead.

The rental craft was moving faster than Amy could have imagined, but it was also shaking badly, its old timbers threatening to come apart. Jake steered around an ancient rowboat in an attempt to use the wallowing dory to block their enemies' progress. To the Cahills' shock, the speedboat plowed right through it, cutting it in half and sending two Khmer fishermen diving for their lives.

That put the Pierce team directly behind them,

closing fast. Galt stood on the bow like a hood ornament, brandishing a spear gun.

"He's going to shoot us!" Atticus wailed.

Galt pulled the trigger, and the projectile was hurtling toward the *Kaoh Kong*. Everybody ducked, even Jake, who left the controls unmanned for a second. But instead of a spear ripping into their hull, a grappling hook sailed over the stern, bit into the wood of the gunwale, and stuck there. Galt's driver cut power, and the line went taut. The two boats were tethered together.

Dan dove for the hook and tried to dislodge it. It wouldn't budge.

"It's no use!" exclaimed Jake, back on the wheel. "We'll never lose them now!"

When the plan occurred to Amy, she saw it perfectly, almost as if an engineer's blueprint had appeared in her brain. She shoved Jake aside, took the wheel, and pushed the boat ahead, full throttle.

"That's what they want us to do!" Jake gasped. "Tow them around until we run out of gas, or fry our engine!"

Her serum-enhanced brain processing data like a computer, Amy built up a head of steam, hauling the speedboat behind them. Then, with sudden violence, she wrenched the helm with all her strength. The wheel snapped from its column and came off in her powerful hands. The *Kaoh Kong* turned suddenly toward the riverbank. This sent the other craft whipping around at incredible velocity. It torqued past the Cahills, swung about, and slammed into a wooden dock. The impact shattered the dock and the boat, sending goons flying in all directions.

The *Kaoh Kong* plowed into the shore, driving halfway up the muddy bank. Amy threw the engine into reverse, but the hull was mired in the wet ground.

Galt's head broke the surface of the water. He was dazed, but alert enough to begin rescuing his companions.

Dan vaulted over the gunwale, sinking ankle-deep. "Let's get out of here!"

"What about the *King Kong*?" quavered Atticus.

"That's Hamilton's problem! It's on *his* credit card!"

The four vaulted up the bank and into the cover of the jungle. Amy led the way, crushing a path through the underbrush with sheer brute strength. Her hallucinations were worse than ever — creatures, grotesque faces lunging out at her from the shadows. Yet the need for escape enabled her to push them aside like the vines she bulldozed through.

Jake, Dan, and Atticus followed without question. It didn't matter where they were going so long as it was away from their pursuers. Crashing sounds and curses behind them indicated that Galt and company were right on their tail.

All at once, from the shaded greenery of the jungle rose a large stone temple. It was nowhere near the size of Angkor Wat. But it was so unexpected that it looked like it had rocketed up from the underworld during some catastrophic seismic event. The group pulled up short, taking in the seven-story spectacle.

"What's that?" panted Dan.

As usual, Atticus was ready with the answer. "Ta Keo," he breathed.

"It looks like a mini Angkor Wat," Dan observed.

"It's built in the same style," Atticus confirmed. "But it's two hundred years older. It doesn't copy Angkor Wat; Angkor Wat copies Ta Keo."

Galt's voice sounded, dangerously close. "Come on! Faster!"

Dan grabbed his friend's arm. "You know your way around this pile of rocks?"

"Not specifically," Atticus admitted. "But Ta Keo is a classic 'temple mountain,' surrounded by two outer walls—"

"Not now, Att!" Jake insisted, pushing his brother from behind. "In case you haven't noticed, you're not lecturing Dad's grad students here!"

As they crashed through the jungle, they reached the west gate of the temple's outer wall.

The serum surged through Amy, heightening her senses. Now it was the Lucian talent for strategy that came to the fore. "If we enter here, we could be cornering ourselves inside Ta Keo. We stand a better chance in the jungle."

"But we have an ace in the hole," Dan countered. "Atticus knows these temples; Galt doesn't."

"You don't understand," she insisted. "*I'm* the one with enhanced—" Before she could finish, a fresh barrage of hallucinations knocked the breath out of her, dropping her where she stood. Scores of angry monkeys came screaming toward her, some swinging on branches and vines, others flying directly through the air.

When it was finally over, Dan was staring down at her in alarm. "All right," she told him. "Let's try it your way."

They rushed up the stairs and entered the grounds via the south portal, passing through the even larger gate there. The majestic temple mountain stood before them, neglected, overgrown, dark, and brooding.

"Note the absence of any decorative carvings," Atticus droned on. "Ta Keo is the only temple in Angkor that was never finished."

The staircase was so steep that it was more like climbing a sandstone ladder.

"Look!" Dan rasped. Galt's blond head and thundercloud brow appeared in the portal of the innermost wall.

"This way! Quick!" Amy ordered. One by one, she pulled them off the steps and shoved them along the narrow terrace in Ta Keo's lowest gallery.

"Did he see us?" Atticus whispered, terrified.

Amy could only shake her head. "Keep moving."

They made their way along the gallery, staying low to take advantage of the cover of the crumbling parapet. Amy risked a glance through an opening in the stone. Galt and his henchmen were crossing the courtyard to the central structure. They were good trackers. She had to give them that. Whatever edge the serum was providing Amy, it was also giving Galt and his goons, although not nearly to the same extent.

Another key difference: I'm the one who's dying.

Pierce's people had been beefing up on "protein shakes," but only she had taken the real thing.

Amy plodded along behind the others, listening to the squelching of their wet shoes on the rock floor and hoping it wasn't as loud as she thought it probably was. Her own sneakers were coated with slimy mud from the riverbank. With each footfall, dark brown sludge was being deposited on the ancient floor, leaving a trail for their pursuers.

She looked down, and watched as a wet blob of slime rolled off her tread and disappeared through a crack in the stone floor.

She froze. A full two seconds later, she distinctly heard the tiny splash of a droplet falling on stone somewhere below her.

Below her?

She was on solid rock, an Angkorian temple mountain! When a drop of moisture oozed into a crack, it stayed there. But Amy knew she'd heard what she'd heard. Her perception had been crazy good since she'd taken the serum. *And a two-second delay before the drip hits bottom means . . .*

"There's a room down there," she said out loud.

A room that just might be their salvation.

CHAPTER 11

Atticus turned to stare at her. "Down where?"

Amy pointed. "Right below us."

"Amy," Jake said urgently, "our dad did his dissertation on Angkor. Att and I have seen fifty different layouts of these temple mountains, including Ta Keo. There's nothing down there but rock."

"In actuality, most of it's feldspathic wacke," Atticus specified. "You know, that greenish sandstone."

Amy almost smiled. "I don't care if it's Grey Poupon. I know I've been having hallucinations. But this isn't one of them. There's open space down there. Now, who's going to help me move these blocks?"

It was a testament to all they'd been through that Dan didn't hesitate. "You'd better be right," he said, kneeling beside her, "because you *are* betting your life—and our lives, too."

The brothers joined them on the ground, and all four set diligently to work cleaning the cracks between the slabs that made up the gallery floor.

Amy dug until her fingers bled. Atticus tapped at

the blocks with a pen, searching for a hollow sound. All they heard were footsteps and gruff voices growing closer. Galt and the goons were already on the stairs.

"Here!" Atticus whispered. "This one!" He jammed the pen into the gap and tried to use it as a lever. But the plastic snapped in two. Jake and Dan, working with their fingers, had more success, but they could not lift the heavy slab more than an inch or two. That much clearance was all Amy needed. She got her hands under the flat stone and heaved it out of the way.

"What was that?" Galt's voice, too close for comfort.

The Cahills peered down into the dark hole they had opened. Steps, carved in the rock, disappeared into total darkness. It was not a very appealing option — just more appealing than waiting for Galt. Down they went, Amy bringing up the rear.

It was narrow and claustrophobic, and they had to hunch their shoulders in order to fit through the shaft. As they descended, Amy reached up and did her best to pull the slab back over the hole. Once it was in place, the blackness was suffocating, and the temperature seemed to drop twenty degrees. When Atticus's metal belt buckle scraped against the sandstone wall, the resulting sparks briefly illuminated their strained faces in the rough-hewn passage. It felt like being trapped in the belly of the earth.

Jake used the flashlight app on his phone to light their way. There was not much to see. The stairs continued down through the rock. *Temple mountain* was an apt name for Ta Keo. They truly had the feeling that they were walking through the heart of a mountain.

"Wait till we tell Dad about this!" Atticus whispered. "We're probably the first people to walk these steps since Angkorian times!"

The stairs ended in a subterranean chamber with a hard-packed dirt floor. The flashlight app played around the small room, casting its glow over stacks of thick-cut bamboo.

Amy's enhanced sense of smell quickly detected something new. "Gunpowder," she said aloud.

"What? Here?" asked Dan. "Why?"

Atticus's nimble mind made the connection. "Fireworks!" he exclaimed excitedly. "The ancient Khmer used them in rituals and celebrations. They learned the technique from Chinese travelers. Look!"

He tipped over one of the bamboo stalks and examined it in cross-section. It had been hollowed out, and its center was packed with powder, now hardened.

Dan was amazed. "You mean, those things are, like, ancient skyrockets?"

Suddenly, flashlight beams crisscrossed the chamber. Before they could react, Galt Pierce stepped down onto the dirt floor. His five thugs halted on the stairs, cutting off any possibility of escape.

With a sinking heart, Amy pictured their muddy sneaker prints on the floor of the gallery above them — *leading straight to the passage here!*

Galt clucked in mock disappointment. "This is a job

for the hired muscle, not the son of the next president. My father overestimated you."

"Your father is out of his mind!" Dan snapped.

"My father is what America needs to get back on top, and you wimps have been sabotaging him since the beginning!" The red flush of rage faded from his fair features, to be replaced by a cruel smile. "Anyway, it all ends here. This is almost too easy."

Amy gathered the others behind her and stepped forward. "It's not going to be as easy as you think." Ever since she had taken the serum, her mind had been playing tricks on her, making it increasingly hard for her to tell the difference between what was real and what was imagined. But at this moment, her priorities were absolutely clear. She might very well die in the next few minutes. That would be fine so long as she got Dan, Jake, and Atticus past the goons and to safety. And that meant fighting all six enemies by herself.

As his sister took an aggressive step toward the son of J. Rutherford Pierce, Dan yanked the belt out from Atticus's jeans and raked the buckle along the sandstone wall, raining sparks all around the room.

Galt was amused. "You're kidding, right? What? Do you think you can set my clothes on fire?"

Dan continued to scrape the buckle back and forth against the wall, sending a blizzard of embers airborne in the dark chamber. Some of these floated down to rest on the stack of ancient fireworks. There was a smoldering smell, followed by a pop and a sizzle. And then a jet of bright color shot from one of the bamboo tubes.

It took Galt's attention from Amy. "What's that?"

"*Down!*" shouted Dan, dropping to the ground and covering his head with his arms.

Amy, Jake, and Atticus followed suit as an explosion of light and color filled the chamber. The fire from the initial rocket set off the others, at first one by one, and then in a subterranean supernova.

The shaft acted as a chimney, drawing the blast up and away from the Cahills on the floor toward the fresh oxygen above. The concussion wave surged through the passage, pushing a wall of color that knocked Galt and his goons off their feet.

It was so bright that Amy had to squeeze her eyes shut. She felt a whirlwind of heat buffet her, scorching her skin and hair. The sound was deafening — like a string of firecrackers going off inside her head. Her only thought was of Dan and the others. Were they all right? Had they managed to cover themselves in time?

And then it was all over, and the silence was as loud as the conflagration had been. The acrid smell of gunpowder hung in the air, but after the onslaught of light and color, it was impossible to make out anything in the darkness.

Jake's flashlight app pierced through the gloom. Amy waved her arms to clear away the smoke that hadn't already been drawn out via the stairs. Galt and the five goons lay draped across the stairs and one another, unmoving.

"Man!" exclaimed Dan, producing his asthma inhaler for a quick puff. "Did anyone get the license plate of that nuke?"

Atticus coughed once and got to his feet. "Those ancient Khmer fireworks were built to last!" His eyes fell on Galt and the goons lying on the stone steps, and his voice grew solemn. "Are they dead?"

Amy leaned over the six victims, pinching out a glowing ember in Galt's fair hair. Her sensitive hearing picked up six distinct pairs of lungs, all breathing. "They're okay, just knocked out by the concussion wave. They may have a few minor burns, too."

"What should we do with them?" Jake mused. "They're still a threat to come after us."

"I vote we hit them over the head with some of that Feldstein wacke," put in Dan.

"Feldspathic," Atticus corrected him.

"I think they'll be unconscious for a while longer," Amy decided. "Let's get out of here."

They stepped around their fallen enemies and climbed the narrow stairs until all four were once again standing on the lower gallery, breathing in great gulps of fresh air. A tour group from Scandinavia watched them quizzically. Who were these young people covered in soot and ash?

"Oh, hey," Jake greeted them genially. "Great temple, huh?"

They left Ta Keo and its grounds as quickly as humanly possible without breaking into a run. As they made their way back through the jungle, Amy struggled hard to conceal the tremors that had returned to her right leg. In fact, all three boys noticed the limp, although no one mentioned it. The triumph of defeating Galt and his thugs faded quickly as they recalled that they were no closer to finding a Tonle Sap water snake.

"We need to push the *King Kong* back on the river," Dan said firmly. "We've still got a couple of good snake-hunting hours before dark."

At that point, the waterway came into view, and the plans changed. Cambodian police swarmed all over the *Kaoh Kong*, and what was left of the wrecked speedboat and shattered dock.

"All we have to do is explain—" Atticus began.

"Don't you open your mouth!" Jake warned. "We'd spend a week in jail before it all got straightened out."

Dan cupped his hands to his mouth. "Hey, officer, look! There's smoke coming from the temple over there! You'd better go check it out."

They followed his pointing finger to the plume rising from the lower gallery. Two of them ran off, jabbering excitedly into walkie-talkies.

Atticus couldn't hold back a grin. "Galt's going to have a lot of explaining to do."

CHAPTER 12

At Trilon Labs in Delaware, Sammy Mourad was working around the clock developing the Franken-serum. In reality, this was not a twenty-four-hour-a-day job.

The guards were not ever to know that Sammy and Nellie had another project going — one that would not have been approved by lab management, and certainly not by J. Rutherford Pierce himself.

Nellie's elbow accidentally nudged the eyedropper, knocking it over the edge of the worktable. When it hit the floor, there was a sound like a miniature thunderclap, and a little flash of light. A wisp of smoke rose to the ceiling. When Nellie went to recover the dropper, there was nothing left of it but the rubber bulb, blackened and melted.

Sammy was as pale as a ghost. "Do you think anybody heard that?"

Nellie quickly scooped up the remains of the dropper and deposited them in the hazardous waste bin. "I don't think so," she said nervously. "Anyway, there's no evidence."

Sammy was terrified. "You can smell the smoke!"

"Lab explosions happen all the time."

"There's nothing combustible in the serum! No one knows we're really" — he dropped his voice to a whisper — *"sterilizing the test tubes."*

Their code again. Sammy and Nellie were spending every extra minute creating nitroglycerin — gallons, dozens of gallons, soon to be hundreds of gallons. When the time was right, this lab, with all its contents, all its research and blueprints and formulas, and, most important, all its serum, was going to the moon.

If a few leftover drips could make that forceful an explosion, it stood to reason that the amount Sammy and Nellie intended to produce could take out the whole lab and the building around it.

But it'll never happen if we get caught before we're ready to put the plan into action! Nellie thought.

They waited breathlessly. No one came, not the guards who regularly looked in on them, nor any of the other scientists or assistants. They were safe.

"We were lucky — this time," Sammy told her, his voice quavering. "People have been laying off us because they like your cooking. But make no mistake about it — we're not their friends; we're their prisoners. One step out of line, and they'll start looking around. And then they'll notice that every spare tank, vat, and container in this lab is full of nitro. We're basically turning the whole facility into one giant bomb! And if they catch us, all the pastries in Paris won't buy us any mercy!"

"Has anyone ever told you you're a real buzzkill?" Nellie asked him.

"I'm just being realistic," he said stubbornly. "There are two of us and dozens of them. You've got to admit our chances of success aren't great."

"We're with Amy and Dan," Nellie told him firmly. "My kiddos can have a *zero* percent chance of success, and they somehow come out on top — *if* they get the kind of support they need." She frowned. She and Sammy had to hold up their end by eradicating not just the serum, but also their enemy's ability to manufacture more.

"You know, there's another way this could go," Sammy added in a hushed tone. "What if we sterilize the test tubes, but we can't get ourselves out before the building goes up?"

"I never said what we're doing isn't dangerous. But that doesn't change the fact that it needs to be done." She held out her hand in the manner of a police officer stopping traffic. In response, Sammy pressed his palm against hers. It had become a signal to the two of them, the silent restatement of a solemn vow. Their goal was to destroy the lab and rejoin Amy and Dan in the fight against Pierce. But if escape turned out to be impossible — if the only way to blow up the serum was to blow themselves up in the process — they had decided it was a sacrifice they were willing to make.

"I know, I know," breathed Sammy. "I'm just nervous, that's all. You can't fault me for that." He checked his watch. "You'd better be getting to the kitchen. Your fans will be expecting their tiramisu for lunch."

She grinned. "Today it's chocolate éclairs."

"Save me one," he said, with a trace of a smile.

Carefully, she and Sammy loaded two five-gallon jugs onto a rolling cart. "Be careful with that stuff," he whispered urgently. "Remember the eyedropper? Think what this much would do."

Nellie made a face. "Let's not, and say we did. How about I just walk slowly and don't bump into anything."

She wheeled gingerly down the hall, pushing the lethal payload in front of her. An armed guard followed a few steps behind.

If he only knew, she thought to herself, unsure if the idea made her want to laugh or cry.

Her destination was storeroom 117A, which had two unique qualities: (1) it was seldom used, and (2) it was located on the building's main gas line, which Nellie privately called Kablooey Avenue.

"Well, now, what have we here?"

Oh, no! It was Dr. Benoit, the senior ranking scientist at the lab.

Nellie fought down the urge to break into a run. The only thing scarier than being busted was the thought of all that nitro, sloshing around inside two five-gallon containers.

"Sorry, Dr. B. Can't stop to chat. Wouldn't want dessert to be late."

The scientist put his foot on one of the containers to stop the cart from moving. "And can the director of research get a little preview of what's on the menu?"

"Oh, this is just liquid sugar," Nellie explained. "It's more concentrated, you know."

He looked delighted. "I haven't had that in years. Give us a taste." He reached for the cap of the nearest container.

If Benoit dipped his finger in the jug, Nellie knew, he was going to get a lot more than a taste of sweet. Without thinking, she lashed out and slapped his hand away.

The guard's eyes widened, his grip tightening on his sidearm. Yet he made no overt move. It was impossible to tell if what he'd witnessed was a playful exchange or something else.

Dr. Benoit looked shocked at first. As the boss of the entire facility, he probably didn't get slapped very often. Then he laughed. "Nellie, you're one of a kind. From now on, I'll wait patiently for your desserts along with everyone else." And he walked off, still chuckling.

The guard's hand retreated from his sidearm.

Nellie wanted to slump over the cart, dry heaving in sheer relief.

But she didn't dare.

CHAPTER 13

The Cahill party got an early start the next morning, grim in the knowledge that time was running out.

Their plan today — as it had been yesterday — was fishing. There were definitely water snakes in the Angkor region, and logic dictated that some of them had to be *Enhydris longicauda*. But like any fishing trip, success would depend on pure random chance. It was a maddeningly flimsy strategy — especially with Pierce closing in on his goals.

Amy had hardly slept at all, and when she had managed to drift off, hideous dreams had woken her quickly. Yet instead of becoming weaker as she got sicker, she was actually becoming stronger. Her slender body began to bulge with muscle tissue. Her face glowed with vitality and strength. She seemed the picture of health when, in reality, she was anything but.

They purchased new fishing nets and hired a *tuk-tuk* to take them out of town. But rather than heading north toward the temples of Angkor, this time they decided to try their luck to the south and the waters of the Tonle Sap, Cambodia's Great Lake.

"Where else would you look for a Tonle Sap water snake?" Dan explained his reasoning. "Tonle Sap is its middle name. Well, Sap, anyway."

Everyone laughed except Hamilton, who had something else on his mind. "The cops left a message on my cell. After the crash, they traced the boat to my credit card. And now I'm a person of interest."

"You're an interesting guy, cuz," said Jonah bitterly. "The crocodile farm seemed pretty interested in *banning you for life*!"

"There might be another avenue we could pursue," Ian began carefully. "Yesterday, I made contact with April May."

This caused a stir in the *tuk-tuk*. The idea that the mythical April May was a real person required a major adjustment in their thinking.

"How?" Dan exclaimed. "Did she e-mail you?"

"No," Ian replied, "she followed me to Angkor Wat and attacked Pony's computer. Hold on to your hats, mates: April May is actually Cara Pierce."

His fellow passengers stared at him in shock.

Hamilton found his voice first. "*The* Cara Pierce?" he asked in amazement. "Like, the daughter of the guy we're doing all this to save the world from?"

As the *tuk-tuk* jounced along the rough roads, Ian recounted the meeting on the grounds of mighty Angkor Wat. The others peppered him with questions, but Amy remained silent, her supercharged brain sifting through the new information at high speed:

April May was the last person any of them expected: the daughter of their enemy. Her involvement meant yet another piece was in play in this vast chess match, a piece no one had anticipated. . . .

Amy spoke up at last. "Why create a secret identity and hire herself out to her dad anonymously?"

"She says she doesn't trust her father anymore, and she wants to work with us to stop him."

"And you believe her!" Amy scoffed. "Do you also believe in the magic rabbit that hides colored eggs every Easter?"

"I don't know, Amy," Dan said slowly. "I think Cara might be legit. I told you how she helped me escape from the Pierce plane."

"That's your hunch," Jake put in. "You can't be totally certain."

"She undid my bonds, and explained exactly how to open the door," Dan insisted. "That's not what they teach you in hostage taking one-oh-one."

"I know she's done a few things to make it seem like she's moving away from her father's side," Amy argued, "but that could be part of a strategy to sucker us in. Does she honestly expect us to accept that she turned herself into the world's greatest hacker and her dad had *no idea*?"

"It's not impossible," Ian supplied. "Every day we hear dozens of stories of people with rich lives online, while their friends and family know nothing about it."

"She's a *Pierce*," Amy said stubbornly.

"And technically a Cahill, too," Ian pointed out. "Her mother's a Starling. I've never been particularly fond of the Ekats. All that tinkering and inventing — so labor-intensive and messy. But she's as closely related to Gideon as any of us. So technically, she wouldn't even be changing sides."

"She'd be double-crossing her own father," Jake argued. "That's not something I would ever do."

"I have some experience with that," said Ian stiffly. "It's by no means easy, but you fight against a parent if that parent is evil. I'd say Pierce qualifies every bit as much as my mother."

The others regarded him in solemnity. They understood how painful it had been for Ian to turn against Isabel Kabra. Knowing he'd made the right choice gave him little comfort, even after all this time.

"We can't trust her," Amy concluded. "And that's just based on what she did as Cara Pierce. How about what she did as April May? She's one of the most ruthless hackers and data thieves in history!"

Dan dug in his heels. "You put me in charge because you didn't trust your own judgment under the serum. Well, how do you know the serum isn't clouding your judgment about Cara?"

"I don't," Amy admitted. "I'm just saying it's too risky."

"But that's a judgment, too!" Dan argued, a little angrily. "If I'm the head of the family, doesn't that mean *I* choose what risks are worth taking?"

"We're betting *my* life, so I make the call on the risks we take."

Dan set his jaw. "And if you're wrong?"

"Then nobody pays a higher price than I do."

There was total silence in the *tuk-tuk* except for the loud raspberry of the three-wheeled vehicle's motor.

Jake put an arm around Amy's shoulder, and she didn't shrug it off.

In the opposite seat, Dan smoldered. Like Jake Rosenbloom had a monopoly on being worried about Amy! From the instant Amy had taken the serum, Dan had realized something that he'd always known, but never put into words: that his greatest fear was losing his sister. Dan had been only four when their parents had died. He had no memory of them, only vague impressions. Amy was everything, had always been everything. And that was even before they'd criss-crossed the globe together and saved each other's lives dozens of times. The one thing in his crazy world that had been as constant as the sun rising in the morning and setting in the evening was that Amy was always there. If he lost her, he was dead certain he would lose himself. The cold fear that had clutched his heart the day she took the serum had been tightening its grip with every passing hour. Jake was a pretty good guy, and his feelings for Amy were genuine. But when it came to worrying about her, he was strictly minor league.

Soon the glassy expanse of the Tonle Sap appeared to the west. As always, Atticus provided the details.

"It's a unique lake, because it swells to almost six times its usual size during the monsoon season. Right now, it's dry season, so it's not very deep — maybe three feet at the most. Another odd feature is that the flow changes direction —"

"Can you tell us anything we actually *need* to know?" Dan interrupted. "Like, is there a Snakes 'R' Us anywhere around here?"

Between Atticus's Khmer and the driver's English, they were able to agree on a drop-off point, a reedy, deserted beach area where the man swore he had seen "many snakes." This was encouraging until Atticus admitted that he wasn't sure of the difference between the words for "many snakes" and "many worms."

"Fine." Amy heaved a sigh. "If we can't complete the antidote, at least we can open a bait shop."

Leaving the *tuk-tuk* driver with instructions to wait for them, they carried their nets down the marshy path to the water's edge. The closer they got, the more the mud sucked at their shoes. Finally, Amy stepped out of her sneakers and continued barefoot.

"Really?" asked Ian as his Gucci loafers sank into the slime. He tried in vain to roll up the pressed cuffs of his designer slacks. "Oh, this is going to be unpleasant."

"Man up, cuz," Jonah called. "If I'm doing it, you're doing it."

They'd crossed the Tonle Sap on their initial journey to Siem Reap, but nothing could have prepared them for the experience of wading into Cambodia's famous Great Lake. It was like a swamp set on simmer. The water was as warm as a Jacuzzi, and teeming with life—insects, and minnows, and algae. The reeds were thick, and as sharp as knives. Every time they dipped their nets into the soup, they came up with at least one catfish, hideous and fighting for its life.

A little downstream, two water buffalo eyed them blandly.

"Yo, bros," Jonah intoned, "don't you dare poop in my lake!"

"How lovely." Ian whimpered.

"Come on, you guys." Amy waded in until she was up to her waist.

There was some resistance, but soon they all fanned out across the murky water, dragging their nets.

"This reminds me of fishing with my family," Hamilton said nostalgically. "It was a lot of fun until Dad punched that manatee and got banned from the national park system."

Atticus ducked himself completely under to avoid a swarm of mosquitoes. In the cloudy water, he saw minnows; floating weeds; several tadpoles; and a long, dark undulating body. He squinted for a better view, comparing the creature to the images of *Enhydris longicauda* they'd seen online. Dark eyes ringing eerily pale pupils . . .

He broke the surface sputtering and gasping for breath. *"Sna-a-a-ke!"*

The response was pandemonium. Everyone converged on Atticus, nets swooping like diving seagulls.

"Where'd he go?" cried Dan.

Ian pointed toward shore. "That way!"

For several minutes, the lake boiled as they scooped, ran, dove, grabbed, and struggled, bumping into each other in an effort to get hold of the phantom snake. Ian butt-ended Hamilton with the net handle, and Jonah took an elbow from Jake. At one point, Dan ducked underwater for a better view and saw nothing but foam as the wild frenzy raged on.

"All right, all right!" Dan shouted, and the activity slowly subsided. "We lost him."

"But it proves something," Jake said excitedly. "That snake is still here somewhere. And if there's one, there must be others." He looked around, earning nods of soggy, panting agreement from his brother, Jonah, Ian, Hamilton, Dan, and — "Where's Amy?"

They did a head count and came up one short. The panic was total. They looked to shore, and then farther out in the lake. Nothing.

Hamilton spied a hint of color breaking the monotonous browns and grays of the Tonle Sap. Orange, the same color as Amy's T-shirt . . .

CHAPTER 14

With a cry of dismay, Hamilton reached down and pulled Amy's unmoving form out of the water. "Over here!" he bellowed, tossing her across his shoulder and making for shore.

If there was a speed record for running through waist-deep water and muddy silt carrying a sixteen-year-old girl on your back, Hamilton Holt shattered it.

"Does anybody know CPR?" Dan asked frantically.

"Don't need it!" Hamilton said briskly. In an instant, he had Amy's limp body turned upside down, holding her by the ankles and shaking her.

"Stop that!" Jake almost screamed. "She's weak! You'll kill her!" He began pounding on Hamilton's back. The big Tomas kept on shaking, and didn't even flinch.

All at once, Amy gurgled and coughed up what looked like a quart of Tonle Sap sludge.

Hamilton flipped her over and stood her on her feet. Amy looked over to where her brother stood, frozen with dread, and flashed him a brave thumbs-up.

Jake was nearly hysterical. "Amy, what happened?"

She shrugged. "One minute we were going after the snake, and the next thing I knew, Hamilton had me by the ankles. No big deal."

"No big deal?!" Jake echoed. "The tremors and hallucinations were bad enough, but this time you blacked out completely! You almost drowned!"

Even the *tuk-tuk* driver was out of his vehicle and looking on in concern. "I take to hospital?" he called.

"Definitely!" Jake confirmed.

"Oh, sure!" Amy retorted. "I'm going to go to a Cambodian doctor and try to explain about a five-hundred-year-old serum!" Her voice broke, and she struggled to regain her composure. She'd nearly died, but that didn't change the fact that she'd die for real if this mission failed. They couldn't let this incident distract them. They simply didn't have the *time*. "And even if we make him understand, he can't do anything about it because there's no antidote—at least, not till we find that snake!"

Jake was not convinced. "All the antidote in the world won't help you if you're already dead."

"That's why we have to get back out there," Dan said, battling to remain all business. "The snake solves everything—the antidote, Amy's health, and J. Rutherford Pierce."

They waved the driver back to his *tuk-tuk*.

This time there was no complaining as the group fanned out across the Tonle Sap and began to dip their nets. The only difference was that now there were three water buffalo wading and watching. The sun continued its climb in the sky, and the temperature rose to the usual afternoon high of "unbearable."

They'd been out there for hours when Dan was startled to hear the *tuk-tuk*'s sputtering engine cough to life. He looked over just in time to see someone handing a wad of US dollars to the driver. A second later, the vehicle made a tight U-turn on the dirt road, and was off and gone.

That was when Dan recognized the burly blond newcomer. He called a warning to the others. *"Galt!"*

Ian was horrified. "Our *tuk-tuk*! How are we going to get back to Siem Reap?"

"That's the least of our problems, yo!" Jonah chimed in. "Look!"

They watched as Pierce's son was joined by his five goons.

"I'm really disappointed in the Cambodian justice system," Hamilton observed with a shake of his crew cut. "How can you practically blow up Ta Keo and be back on the street the very next day?"

"You talking about them or us?" quipped Jonah. The comment carried little of his famous hip-hop attitude.

"What are they going to do to us?" Atticus asked fearfully.

He soon had his answer, although he might have preferred to be kept in suspense. Their expressions menacing, Galt and his henchmen waded into the Tonle Sap after their prey.

The Cahills had a seven to six advantage in numbers, but their enemies were all enhanced by the serum, five of them adults. Amy's Lucian boost instantly took stock of their situation. "I'll fight three of them. The rest of you team up and protect each other."

"Amy, you're in no condition for this," Jake warned.

"Are you kidding?" she snapped back. "This is the only thing I *am* in condition for!"

The Rosenbloom brothers hunkered together, so Dan sidled over to Jonah and Ian for safety. His primary attention, though, was on Amy. She had been more aggressive since the serum, but never had she looked so dangerous. Her eyes, little more than slits, locked on Galt with the deadly concentration of a cheetah about to pounce.

Galt didn't notice any of this. He was harboring very hard feelings over yesterday's events on the river, in Ta Keo, and later at the police station. There he had been grilled for eight hours before his father had wired over a sizable bribe to buy his freedom. He was beyond rage.

"You must think you're pretty hot stuff," he sneered, staring straight at Amy. "Like, 'No one can touch us. We're the Cahills. We're special.' Well, let me tell you something—"

That was as far as he got. Amy sprang at him with astonishing suddenness, flattening him with an elbow

to the face. He went down with a splash, disappearing below the surface. She put a knee on the top of his
head, holding him under. It took all his strength to
fight his way back to the surface.

At that point, the other five attacked, and the battle
was on. Two of them rushed to Galt's defense. Amy
knocked one back with a kick to the ribs, and held the
other at bay with a stiff-arm.

Hamilton traded blows with his serum-enhanced
opponent, giving as good as he got. But Ian was in
trouble. He had learned boxing in his English board-
ing school, and his style was all about rules and fair
play. The trained henchman landed a vicious kick in
the center of Ian's chest that knocked the air out of the
teenager's lungs and left him flat on the muddy lake
bottom. Jonah threw himself around the man's neck,
and was shrugged off as easily as a grasshopper. Dan
broke his fishing net over the goon's head, which didn't
even slow him down.

Ian rose from the water, determined to fight in a
more Lucian style. In his hands, he grasped one of the
large, slow-moving Mekong catfish. Clutching the fish
like a cricket bat, he took a mighty swing and landed
a low blow across the man's kidneys. Their opponent
did not go down, but as he lurched forward, all three
Cahills jumped on his back and held on for dear life.

Clamped on and hanging there, Dan caught
a glimpse of his sister in a boxing match with Galt
and two others. He allowed himself to consider the

possibility, just for a fleeting second, that they might actually get through this.

"Sto-o-op!"

There was something in the desperation, the sheer panic in the voice that made everyone freeze, even in the midst of battle.

There stood Jake, his face streaming with blood and mud. "Don't fight! We can't! He'll kill Att!"

Behind him, the last of the goons was holding something underwater. For the purpose of illustration, the man raised his arm so they could all see. The "object" in his fist was Atticus's dreadlocks. The terrified boy choked and gasped for air.

"I'll do it, you know!" the man roared. He forced Atticus under again in a brutal demand for their surrender. "You've got five seconds to give it up, or you'll never see your freaky little friend alive again!"

With one hand, Amy grabbed a fistful of Galt's shirt, heaved him away from his defenders, and forced him under. "I don't see any gills on Junior!" It was a spectacular feat of strength, one that could only have come from Gideon Cahill's original creation.

The goon holding Atticus didn't flinch. Bubbles began to rise from the water in front of him.

The cry from Jake was barely human. "Amy, please don't do this!"

It took Dan's voice to penetrate the shell of cold purpose that had Amy in its grip. "Amy, stop it! I *order* you to give it up!"

It was the first time Dan had ever used those exact words—*I order you.* It felt wrong, but there was an instant result. He was the head of the Cahill family, issuing a direct command. Amy pulled the sputtering Galt out of the water and released him. Hamilton stopped resisting, and held up his hands in surrender. One by one, Jonah, Ian, and Dan jumped off their goon. Then and only then did Atticus's captor free the half-drowned boy. Sobbing and spitting, Atticus staggered forward, wheezing in gulps of air. His brown skin, smeared with mud, had turned an almost bluish color. It was obvious that he could not have held out much longer.

The fight was over, the battle lost.

As soon as Galt was back on his feet, he threw a punch at Amy, who took it square on the chin and didn't even blink.

"You're going to pay for what you did to us!" he growled. To his henchmen, he called, "Let's get out of this cesspool. But watch them. They're tricky."

Galt and his men rounded up the Cahills in the waist-deep water and began to push them toward the shore. Jonah took a rough shove and swallowed an angry *yo watch it!* There was no point in resisting now. Their enemies had proved they had the weapon that was always supreme—not just the ability to kill, but also the willingness to do it.

Then he saw the log floating in the reeds, and realized that he might have a weapon, too. He had seen many logs like that the previous day—and none of them had been logs.

The international pop star probed the silty bottom with his foot until he found a stone slightly larger than a golf ball. Digging with his toes, he lifted it out of the water and transferred it to his right hand. Taking careful aim—he was an artist, not a baller—he reared back and let fly. The rock bounced off the log with a dull thud, and plopped into the lake.

The goon shoved him again. "Whoa! What do you think you're doing?"

Jonah didn't answer. With a mixture of satisfaction and dread, he noted that the "log" was no longer floating there.

A shriek was torn from Galt's throat as the twelve-foot crocodile rose in front of him in a violent shower.

Instantly, they were transformed from captors and captives to thirteen people running for their lives. Amy took advantage of the chaos to smash Galt in the chin with the open heel of her hand. The blow sent him sprawling in the opposite direction of the shore. He went down in white water churned up by snapping jaws. As the Pierce henchmen scrambled to rescue him, the Cahills fled for the beach. The seven pounded onto dry land, scooped up their shoes, and sprinted for the road.

"How are we going to get away from here?" Ian wailed. "Our *tuk-tuk* is gone!"

At that very moment, a black Humvee roared up the

road, its driver masked by a balaclava. A single motion invited them to jump in.

"Who are you?" Amy challenged.

The driver repeated the hand gesture, with increased urgency. This time, all seven began to clamber aboard, no questions asked. The Pierce team was very close now. Galt's fist slammed down on the hood of the Humvee. One of the henchmen stepped around him and reached for Atticus. Hamilton got a hand under the eleven-year-old's arm just as the driver stomped on the gas. The Humvee reversed up the dirt road, its spinning wheels spitting mud and stones in all directions. Hamilton dragged Atticus inside and dumped him into his brother's lap.

At top speed, the military jeep backed into a small clearing and spun around. As they roared down the road in the direction of Siem Reap, they passed a boxy van that must have been Galt's transportation. It sat low on its axles. All four tires had been slashed.

"You're very thorough," Amy commented, still suspicious.

The driver pulled off the balaclava and tossed it out into the jungle. Long blond hair tumbled about her shoulders.

"Now do you trust me?" asked Cara Pierce.

"Cara!" Ian exclaimed.

The revelation was nearly as mind-boggling as the other events of the day. Amy blinked to assure herself this wasn't another of her serum-induced hallucinations.

"Whoa!" breathed Jonah. "This is messed up, yo!"

"But thanks," put in Jake. "You probably saved all our lives."

"Especially mine," added Atticus in a small voice. "I think your brother's figured out that I'm the weakest link."

Dan had been right, Amy reflected. Ian, too. At some point, all the others had been willing to entertain the idea that not all of Cara's loyalties lay with her father and brother. Amy had been the lone holdout.

And I'll hold out still, she raged inwardly. *Just because Cara isn't 100 percent pro-Pierce doesn't put her on our side!*

"Galt's not the real problem," Cara informed them.

"He was a pretty big problem five minutes ago," said Amy coldly.

"What I'm trying to say," Cara persisted, "is that if we stop my dad, everything else will fall into place. Galt's just an insecure kid trying to please a father who can't be pleased. The others are hired muscle. They'll go away as soon as the paychecks stop coming. And when we complete that antidote, the serum won't be an issue anymore."

Amy's eyes narrowed. "Unless I miss my guess, you're pretty juiced up yourself."

"Guilty," Cara admitted. "But I quit. I'll never touch that stuff again." She glanced sideways at Amy. "And I recommend you do the same. I doubt those muscles are from lifting weights."

"Funny that the Pierce family is suddenly so interested in my well-being," said Amy bitingly.

"Because I've been having some bad reactions," Cara went on. "And I know my dad is hiding his own symptoms. The antidote will fix all that, right?"

Amy cast a murderous look around the Humvee, commanding everyone's silence.

"Okay, I get it," Cara sighed. "No more questions."

Dan spoke up. "I've got one for you. What does Pierce want the antidote for? He wouldn't take it even if he had it. His whole plan is the opposite—using the serum to make him and his people unstoppable."

"He thinks he can use it to develop a kind of super-serum," she explained, "with all the benefits, but none of the side effects. Also, he wants to keep the antidote away from you. You could use it to turn his supermen back into ordinary people, himself included. That's why we need each other. You've got the antidote, and I've got the inside access. We can do this, but only together."

"There's a problem," Dan confessed. "Well, actually, there are about twenty problems, but the biggest is we don't have the antidote. We're still short one ingredient."

"The venom of the Tonle Sap water snake," Cara concluded.

The exhilaration of their incredible escape withered as the true result of the mission began to sink in. No snake. No antidote.

For Amy, the failure was stingingly personal. Another precious day had been squandered out of the meager handful she had left. And they were no closer to either prolonging her life or thwarting Pierce. It was a total lose-lose.

Ian held up a mud-encrusted Gucci loafer. "Ruined," he said tragically. "The nubuck leather will never be the same again. Who knows what the local shops will offer as replacements. Flip-flops, no doubt."

He tried to jam a wet foot into one of the loafers, but withdrew it with a look of distaste. "There's something slimy in there." He held up the shoe and peered inside. A sleek dark head emerged, dark eyes encircling telltale pale pupils. A white mouth opened impossibly wide, revealing a forked tongue and tiny fangs. The head lunged at him suddenly; one of the fangs scratched his nose.

"Ow!" He dropped the shoe, and the hitchhiker darted out.

It was a small Tonle Sap water snake.

With the final ingredient swimming circles in a water jug in the back of the Humvee, the next order of business was what to do about Cara Pierce. Dan and Ian trusted her, and the others were inclined to take their side. Amy was the lone holdout. And just as the serum had enhanced her physical performance, it had boosted her stubbornness as well.

In the end, she agreed that Cara would come back to their guesthouse to discuss possible cooperation, but only if Amy's conditions were met: (1) She would surrender her phone, and the GPS chip would be removed and destroyed. (2) She would be blindfolded until they were indoors so she could not betray their location. And (3) she would be handcuffed and restrained while she was with them.

"Oh, come on, Amy!" Dan exploded. "No way she's going to agree to that!"

"I agree to all of it," Cara said readily. "Amy's just being careful. I don't blame her a bit. If I were in her shoes, I'd be the same way."

As it turned out, handcuffs were not readily available in the stores of Siem Reap. But Amy was able to improvise with a dog leash. She made a great show of cinching Cara's hands behind her back and then fastening her to an iron pipe.

"Come on, Amy, that's too tight," Ian complained. "She's betraying her whole family to help us. I know better than anyone how hard that can be. And how do we repay her? With medieval torture."

"I'm fine," Cara assured him. "But you might want to do something about your nose. It looks a little irritated where the snake got you."

Ian ran to the bathroom and looked in the mirror. It was true. The site of the scratch was an angry red. And was that swelling? "I've been bitten by a poisonous snake!"

"You said it was only slightly poisonous," Dan reminded him.

"Oh, that's a tremendous comfort!" Ian snapped back. "When the venom reaches my brain stem, you are slightly disinvited to my funeral."

"It only nicked you," Hamilton added.

"Good thing I'm surrounded by medical experts!" Ian spat sarcastically. He ran over to Pony's laptop for snakebite research.

Jake's priorities were definitely elsewhere. "I know I'm not a Cahill, but this seems like a no-brainer to me. We have all the ingredients. We should make the antidote and give it to Amy before she gets any worse."

"It doesn't work that way," Amy told him, finally taking the time to kick off her muddy sneakers and collapse onto one of the rush mats. "We can't just mix it up in a bucket and boil it over an open fire. It has to be done in a lab, with a real chemist."

"Sammy Mourad," Cara put in.

Amy all but pounced on her. "What do you know about Sammy?"

"I know my father has him at his Delaware facility. I assume you've got Cahill assets already working on getting him out."

A fierce look. "Nice try." No one had been able to reach Nellie for a few days. Amy was beginning to suspect something had gone wrong, but she certainly wasn't going to express that to Cara.

"Here it is!" Ian exclaimed from the depths of Pony's laptop. "'How to treat the bite of *Enhydris longicauda*, the Tonle Sap water snake.'" He read avidly. "Harmless? Easy for them to say! It's not *their* nose!"

The door burst open, and Dan and Atticus marched in. Atticus waved a glass jar in triumph. "We got bugs!"

"What for?" Hamilton asked, mystified.

"Snake food," Dan explained enthusiastically. "You don't want him to die before we can get his venom."

"We've got beetles, roaches, and ants," Atticus added proudly. He frowned at the glass jar. "Uh-oh. I think the beetles and roaches ate some of the ants." He and Dan rushed over to the jug that was serving as their snake habitat, and began dropping wriggling insects into the water.

"Look!" breathed Atticus. "He's hungry!"

Jake shook his head, half-amused, half-disgusted.

"He's a college student at age eleven, his IQ is off the charts, and what makes him happy? Feeding cockroaches to a snake."

Next in the door was Jonah, his expression grim. "Bad news, yo. The jet can't get here till tomorrow."

"Why not?" Amy demanded. "It's only in Phnom Penh."

The pop star hung his head. "Uh-uh. Newfoundland."

"What's it doing there?" Jake demanded.

"Saving whales. Or seals. You know those Hollywood types. They love that Greenpeace stuff."

"Yeah, but why are they flying in *your* plane?" Dan asked, mystified.

Jonah looked embarrassed. "Now that I'm not touring anymore, I figured I could make a few bucks by renting out the G6 when I don't need it."

"But you *do* need it!" Jake almost wailed. "You've never needed it so badly in your life!"

Jonah shrugged miserably. "Tomorrow. Best they can do. They'll be in Siem Reap by noon."

A babble of protest went up in the guesthouse.

Amy put a stop to it. "We're Cahills. If we can't change it, we deal with it. It's only another day."

Her red-rimmed eyes met Jake's. The question hung unspoken in the air between them.

How many days did Amy have left?

CHAPTER 16

Cara Pierce wasn't sleeping very well, which was not at all surprising. When your wrists were bound behind you, and your shoulders were coming out of their sockets, and an iron pipe was pressed against the center of your back, it made it pretty hard to relax.

She wasn't sure she deserved much better. *Traitor.* She'd turned her back on her own flesh and blood, and thrown her chips in with her father's worst enemies. A dictionary definition of *treason.*

But it's the right thing to do, she reminded herself.

She'd monitored her father's activities, both as his daughter and as her cyber alter ego, April May. J. Rutherford Pierce had gone over to the dark side, to use Star Wars parlance. Somewhere along the line, construction had become destruction, and ambition had turned poisonous.

One memory continued to haunt her. The palatial mansion on Pierce Landing had been brand-new, so Cara must have been eleven or twelve. Dad was at his desk, poring over schematic drawings, the paper crackling as he turned the large pages. Designs of new printing presses, he told her, for his many newspapers and magazines.

There was something in his eyes when he said that—like he was lying, but it didn't matter. It was all a big game, *his* game.

She never questioned him, not because she had no questions, but because she didn't dare. She saw the way other grown-ups treated her father—with respect. With *fear*. It wasn't that J. Rutherford Pierce couldn't lie; it was more like when he did it, it didn't count as lying, because he *owned* the truth.

Fast-forward to last year, when Cara saw those "printing presses" again—this time in her advanced-placement physics textbook. She was so brainwashed that she actually raised her hand and said the words aloud in the classroom: "Printing presses."

The chorus of laughter from her fellow students still resounded in her ears.

The teacher frowned at her. "Read the caption, Miss Pierce."

Ears burning, Cara examined the page.

Those drawings had never had anything to do with newspapers or printing. They were engineering diagrams for the trigger of a nuclear bomb.

What's the real treason? Turning your back on your father, or on the whole world?

The others were sleeping, albeit fitfully. Small

wonder after the day they'd put in. The rush mats kicked up a lot of noise as they tossed and turned. Ian was snoring, probably due to the swelling of his snake-bit nose. He was adorable with that schnoz. She hoped not too much of the snake's venom had been wasted. There were plans for it. Big plans.

The most restless of the sleepers was Amy. From the moment she'd closed her eyes, she had been tossing and whimpering through what must have been a series of hideous nightmares. Cara had a pretty good idea of what that was like. She'd been experiencing it, too, although not as intensely as what Amy appeared to be suffering. She was thrashing, hyperventilating, shivering. At one point, she sat bolt upright, bathed in sweat, and spoke words that made no sense.

In spite of everything, Cara could not help but pity her. Clearly, her serum dose had been much more powerful than anything Cara had taken, even when she'd been swapping protein shakes with Galt.

She leaned as close to Amy as she could, and tried to sound reassuring. "You're okay. It's only a dream."

Amy quieted down and went back to sleep.

It was a little disconcerting, but Cara reassured herself that Amy had never actually awoken. With an ease that would have astonished the Cahills, she squeezed her wrists into an impossible shape and slipped out of the leash. She got to her feet, stretched once, and surveyed the sleepers. The coast was clear.

She tiptoed through the mats and picked up the jug

that held the Tonle Sap water snake. Like a phantom, she was out of the room and gone without a sound.

Jake had always been an early riser. Growing up the son of a renowned archaeologist, he had spent much of his childhood up at first light to rush off with his father to some new discovery or dig. So it was not surprising that he was the first one awake the next day.

Every morning was the same lately. Jake would enjoy three or four seconds of blissful ignorance, and then he would remember: Amy was dying. It was like getting the same devastating news again on a regular basis. Next came the calculation. How long since she'd taken the serum? How much time did she have left? It had been five days since she'd downed the contents of that fateful bottle. She might have as little as forty-eight hours left.

But now there was a new wrinkle. They had the final ingredient. The antidote was no longer a matter of "if," but "when." It was a race against the clock, but she would make it. She had to. And then—maybe—they'd be able to pick up where they'd left off.

With a yawn, he looked over in her direction. His heart very nearly jumped through his rib cage, clean out of his chest. The problem wasn't Amy. She was still fast asleep on her mat. But beside her, the leash hung loose from the black iron pipe.

Cara Pierce was gone.

His neck snapped around, his eyes searching for the water-jug snake habitat.

It wasn't there.

"Everybody up!" He tried to bellow, but it came out more like a gasp. "Wake up! Up!"

In an instant, they were all up on their feet, bleary-eyed but alert. It was a testament to the knife-edge they'd been living on.

"Cara escaped, and she stole the snake!"

The effect was like yelling *Fire!* in a crowded room. There was a mad scramble and, in seconds, everyone was dressed and ready to go. But what the course of action should be was unclear.

"We'll find her!" Dan raged. "We'll tear the town apart, plank by plank!"

Ian's features radiated an intense heat that had nothing to do with the Cambodian climate. "I *vouched* for her! I convinced you all to trust her! A Lucian should know better," he said bitterly.

"It's *my* fault," Amy lamented. "I should have stuck with my first instincts."

They went on in this way, beating themselves up, and issuing dark threats of revenge. They were so wrapped up in their distress that they barely noticed when the door opened and in walked Cara Pierce.

"Morning, you guys. What's all the excitement?"

The group watched in mute amazement as she set down a rectangular glass aquarium with a carrying handle. Inside swam their Tonle Sap water snake, spry and healthy. Cara then returned to her spot, wriggled her hands deftly back into the leash, and sat down on the floor, leaning against the iron pipe.

She looked up with an innocent smile. "You didn't think you could keep me locked up, did you?"

"Where were you?" Amy demanded.

"At the pet store. We need a decent habitat for the snake if we intend to take it halfway around the world. Then I dropped in on my brother to make sure he doesn't put out an all-points bulletin for me."

"Did you tell him where we are?" Dan probed.

Cara showed a flash of exasperation. "Have you been listening to anything I've said? I don't want my dad to win! I want *you* to win! I want *us* to win!"

Jake was still shaken and angry. "And you think you're going to earn our trust by sneaking out?"

"No. By coming back."

Amy reached behind her and undid the leash. "You've made your point. So you say you can help us. How?"

Cara gathered them close. "You're in a position to start making the antidote. But the trick is going to be finding a way to deliver it to my dad and all his enhanced people at the same time."

Amy nodded. "Keep talking."

Cara smiled. "Let me tell you a story about a clambake. . . ."

CHAPTER 17

Sammy poked his head in through the swinging door and spied Nellie scrubbing the spotless kitchen. "What are you doing?"

She didn't even look up. "I like to leave my work-space in perfect condition."

Frowning, he tossed a glance over his shoulder at the guard who was waiting in the hallway.

He approached her and whispered a single word in her ear: "Why?"

"I take pride in my kitchen," she said through clenched teeth.

"No one's going to see it," he insisted in a low voice. "There's enough nitro to blow up a medium-size air-craft carrier. No one will know how clean it was before it was vaporized."

"*I'll* know," she said, and kept on polishing.

Sammy grew stern. "We need to get to the lab. This is the biggest night of our lives. And unless everything goes perfectly, it'll be the last one, too."

She did not meet his eyes. "Don't you see that, if I

don't keep myself occupied, I'll wimp out before we can put the plan into action?"

"You're not going to wimp out," Sammy said firmly. "You're the strongest person I know. Now, let's get to the lab. We have less than half an hour before lockdown."

It was their nightly routine, well known by their captors. Nellie would finish in the kitchen, and then go to help Sammy tidy up the lab at the end of the day. Shortly thereafter, guards would take them to their separate cells, several levels below, and lock them inside.

Except that nothing would be routine about tonight.

As they navigated the corridors, they received friendly greetings from several staff members. It was amazing how a few really awesome desserts could turn captors and captives into colleagues and companions. Even the guard trailed behind them at a respectful distance, his weapon holstered. And when they entered the lab, he hung back in the corridor.

"I just hope everybody makes it out in time," Nellie whispered to Sammy. "Just because they work for someone evil doesn't make them evil, too."

"Forget *them*," Sammy countered. "I hope *we* make it out. Because once we start the chain reaction, this operation doesn't have a pause button." He peered into her eyes, and she remembered how hot she'd found him the first time they'd met—back when *hot* had another meaning besides a thousand pounds of nitro waiting to go off. "Nellie, I have to say this now, because I might not ever get another chance. It's been horrible being a prisoner here. But I wouldn't trade a minute of it, because it's where I got to know you."

Nellie planted a tiny kiss on the end of his perfect nose. "To be continued," she promised, wishing this could be more of a romantic moment. But there was too much ahead of them, too much that could go wrong. And no matter how she sliced and diced the possibilities in her mind, an alarmingly high proportion of them left Sammy and Nellie lying dead at the bottom of a pile of rubble. "Now, let's do this."

A nitro bomb hidden in the fire extinguisher in the lab would serve as the trigger. Once it blew, the explosion would travel through the building via the gas lines, setting off the dozens of caches of nitro strategically placed where they would do the most damage. In a very short time, there would be no serum left, and no building, either. Most important, all notes, drawings, and formulas regarding Gideon Cahill's creation would be incinerated.

A small charge was attached magnetically to the extinguisher. Sammy set the delay for three minutes, and paused. "Together?" he asked Nellie.

Their thumbs met on the button and they pressed. The readout jumped from 3:00 to 2:59 and began counting down. There was no turning back now.

The two donned breathing masks. Sammy climbed up on an experiment table and held a small flask directly under the poison detector on the ceiling. He popped the stopper, and a wisp of sarin gas was drawn up into the unit. Instantly, alarms howled throughout the building. An automated voice boomed out of the PA system.

"Contamination alert! Evacuate immediately!"

Sammy jumped down and they burst into the corridor, which was already filled with agitated staff members. In a vast lab filled with chemicals, a contamination alert was nothing to be ignored. Where was the guard? Had he abandoned his post?

Sammy pointed. There he was, searching the turbulent throng for a supervisor and instructions. He looked uncertain, but—bad sign—his gun was drawn. At last, he reversed course and came racing toward the lab.

The prisoners ducked into the men's room.

"He has no breathing mask," Nellie whispered in alarm.

"The gas has dissipated by now," Sammy assured her.

They watched through a crack in the door as the man disappeared into the lab. Finding no one, he reemerged, and ran off in another direction. The two dropped their own masks and counted off another ten seconds as the sirens blared on.

"Contamination alert! Evacuate immediately!"

When they ventured into the hall, the crowd of staff members had thinned considerably as everyone made for the exits. Sammy and Nellie dashed off against the flow of evacuees, toward the complex's main office suites. A few of the scientists tried to warn them they were headed the wrong way, but it was out of concern for their safety rather than an attempt to keep them prisoner. They were free — at least as free as they could be while trapped in the basement of a building that was about to blow sky high.

The alarm resounded in the stairwell.

"Contamination alert!"

Sammy glanced at his watch for a time check. "Two minutes!" he called to Nellie. She nodded and kept on moving. They were right on schedule, but it was going to be tight.

At the main basement level, the halls were deserted and the wail of the siren swirled around them, echoing off the walls. Nellie broke into a sprint, but slowed as Sammy began to fall behind. They had dreamed up this plan together, made it a reality together, and set it in motion together. And now they would be going out together — or not at all.

"One minute!" Sammy panted behind her.

Nellie wheeled around a corner, and their destination beckoned at the end of the long corridor — the luxurious suite of offices. She dashed for it, with Sammy perhaps ten yards behind. They were going to make it!

A strong arm reached out and grabbed her around the neck, stopping her progress so suddenly that she almost strangled. "Going somewhere, missy?" came a smooth, oily voice over the din of the alarm.

She recognized her attacker immediately. Dr. Jeffrey Callender, the lab's physician and the founder of the Callender Institute, where Fiske Cahill was being "treated."

"Let her go!" boomed Sammy.

"Oh, I don't think so," Callender replied in a falsely pleasant tone. "It wouldn't take much for me to snap her lovely little neck. I'm a doctor, after all." He looked down at Nellie. "Such a shame that would be. I've become rather fond of your pastries."

"We've all got to get out of here!" she shrilled. "Can't you hear the alarm?"

"Yes, but since you two are running in the opposite direction, I assume you know something nobody else does."

Sammy blanched. "As I suspected." Callender was triumphant. "The alarm is cover for your pathetic little escape attempt. Or perhaps something else? There's no exit here. . . ."

"For God's sake, let us go!" Sammy roared. "The whole building's set to explode in thirty seconds!"

"You must think I'm really stupid—" the doctor began.

"You *are* really stupid!" Nellie howled. Channeling all her strength, she pulled her right hand free and sucker-punched him in the face. Enraged, Callender reached for her again, and Nellie understood that if she allowed him to recapture her, it would mean the end of her life. She might ultimately win the fight—but not before the entire complex went up in a fireball.

With a grunt of anger and purpose, she rammed

her shoulder into her opponent's chest. As he staggered back, Nellie brought up her foot in a karate kick and landed a direct hit on the long nose. There was a sickening crunch of shattering cartilage, accompanied by Callender's howl of agony.

Sammy was upon him in an instant. Not trusting his boxing skills, the young scientist drove the top of his head into Callender's chin. The doctor dropped where he stood, dazed.

A little dazed himself, Sammy checked the time. "Ten seconds!"

They raced down the hall and into Dr. Benoit's office. As they burst through the door, Sammy pulled a small remote control from his pocket. It was programmed to set off another nitro bomb—the smallest they had created. The charge was hidden beneath the leaves of a potted plant sitting on a high shelf against the wall—a *foundation* wall.

He pressed the button and they braced themselves for the blast that would breach the corner of the foundation, collapse the bricks above it, and open up an escape route from the complex.

Nothing happened.

Sammy pressed again and again with no result. The remote had failed, and there was no time left to tinker with it. The three minutes had ticked away. Brilliant as it was, their plan had been undone by its smallest component.

We're going to die.

Strangely, facing the end, Nellie's first thought wasn't of Sammy or even herself. It was of her beloved kiddos, Amy and Dan, and the awful fact that she'd never bail them out of trouble again. . . .

The first explosion rocked the building, followed by a roaring sound as the gas lines ignited and the planned disaster spread. They could feel the wall of heat building behind them and picture the column of flame that surged through the building, destroying everything in its path.

In a last-ditch effort to save their lives, Nellie picked up the paperweight from Benoit's desk and hurled it at the plant. The heavy glass struck the bottle of nitro, smashing it into a million pieces. The unstable chemical compound went off, blowing a hole in the wall the size of an SUV. An avalanche of rubble rained down — fragments of bricks and concrete, a blizzard of plaster dust, earth, and grass.

Sammy and Nellie climbed the mound of earth and debris, eyes stinging from the smoke and soot. Through the dense fog twinkled a single star —

The outside world!

Legs pumping like pistons, Sammy and Nellie scrambled up from of the steaming office, hit level ground, and began to run. Direction was not important; only distance mattered.

When the fire in the building reached the dozens of caches of nitro spread along Kablooey Avenue, a series of mammoth blasts assaulted their eardrums and lit up the night around them. It was like a string of firecrackers, only each individual bang was a spectacular detonation. A second or two later, the wreckage began to pelt down around them—bricks, wood, furniture, equipment, and a blizzard of burning embers.

Still they ran, grateful to be alive, and hoping to stay that way.

"Look out!" Sammy took hold of Nellie's shoulders and jerked her violently to the left. A heavy centrifuge slammed into the space she'd occupied a split second before.

A burning clamp struck Sammy in the back, nearly knocking him flat on his face. Without missing a step, Nellie beat out a small fire on his lab coat.

When at last she risked a quick glance over her shoulder, an appalling sight met her eyes. The Trilon Laboratory complex had vanished as if it had never existed. In its place was a charred, slag-and-scrap-filled crater, still ablaze. If an asteroid had struck the Delaware countryside right here, it could not have done any more damage.

"I guess those test tubes are"—her breath came in gasps—"pretty darn sterilized right about now!"

"Do you think everybody made it out?" Sammy panted.

"Everybody but Callender! Come on! When the cops get here, we need to be long gone!"

As they sprinted for the cover of the trees, they passed a large piece of steel debris that had been thrown more than three hundred yards from the building. Nellie recognized it immediately. It was a piece of her kitchen counter — dented, singed, but spotlessly clean.

CHAPTER 18

"This is Siem Reap center calling private aircraft P-JW en route from Gander, Newfoundland. . . . You are not cleared for landing. Repeat: *not* cleared. Please acknowledge."

In the tower, the air traffic controller sat at his radar screen watching the flashing dot that was the approach of a Gulfstream G6 belonging to international super-star Jonah Wizard. The man's attention was divided between the monitor in front of him and the teenager standing directly behind him — Galt Pierce.

"Negative," crackled the reply from Jonah's pilot. "My approved flight plan is from Gander to Siem Reap."

"No!" Galt's voice crackled with electricity. His father was counting on him to keep that plane from landing. This was Galt's big chance to regain his right-ful place as Dad's favorite. "Tell him to go someplace else!"

Obediently, the controller radioed, "Please divert to Phnom Penh or Bangkok. You are *not* cleared for approach."

"I'm nonstop from Newfoundland," the pilot replied, "running low on fuel. Must land to gas up. Over."

In answer, Galt thrust his cell phone to the controller's ear.

"Listen, you steaming backwater traffic cop!" roared the angry voice on the other end of the line. "This is J. Rutherford Pierce speaking! Do you recognize that name, or do I have to tap it out in code with two coconuts?"

"Sir!" the man exclaimed in a frightened whisper. "I cannot send away an aircraft that's in need of fuel! It's against every international agreement!"

"The only nation you need to agree with is the good old US of A! You'll understand that better when *I'm* president. Now send that plane away!"

Trembling now, the controller spoke into his microphone. "You are not cleared, P-JW. Please divert as directed."

"No can do, Siem Reap Tower," the pilot returned. "I'm coming in. Requesting runway assignment."

"No runway assignment!" bellowed Pierce over the phone.

"Dad, I got this!" cried Galt, determined to make the most of this opportunity to step up in his father's eyes. He turned to the controller. "No runway assignment!"

"I am sorry, P-JW," the man began, haunted. "I regret to inform you that the Siem Reap Airport will not accommodate you—"

Then it happened. The lights went out in the control tower. All computers and radar screens went dark. The intercoms fell silent.

"What's going on?" Galt demanded.

"We have lost power!" the controller exclaimed in alarm. "This has never happened before!"

"Fix it!" shouted Pierce through the phone.

The man ran to an electrical panel and began flipping switches, but to no avail. "I don't understand. The runway lights are illuminated. The terminal is fine. Power is everywhere — except here in the tower!"

"Well, *I* understand!" came a roar from the phone. "You've been hacked, you clown!"

Galt felt cold panic. None of this was his fault, but if the mission failed, he'd get blamed anyway. "Call April May!" Galt sputtered. "She can undo this!"

Outside, Jonah's jet skimmed low over the horizon and set down on Runway Two.

"The plane!" croaked Galt. "Do something! Impound it!"

The controller shrugged helplessly. "I have no such authority."

"The Cahills!" Even through the handset, Pierce's rage was palpable. "Get out there, Galt! Stop them — even if you have to tackle the pilot and sit on him!"

"Got it, Dad!" Galt raced for the exit and nearly knocked himself unconscious. The swinging door would not budge. Dazed, he turned to the controller. "Why won't it open?"

"My access panel is not operating. We must be in lockdown mode."

"Why?"

"I think perhaps your father is correct," the man informed him solemnly. "We have been hacked."

Under cover of the jungle just beyond the runway, Cara leaned over her keyboard, her fingers flying. "You guys better move it," she told the Cahills. "I can't keep the tower dark forever."

They watched the jet taxi toward them and stop in close proximity, as if it had been summoned like a pet dog. The door opened and the copilot appeared.

The Cahill group ventured out of the trees.

"Is everybody okay, boss?" the man asked Jonah.

"It's all good," Jonah replied, "so long as we bounce before the tower powers back on."

"We need to take on fuel if we're going to make it all the way to the States," the copilot informed him seriously.

"No can do," Jonah replied. "Siem Reap's too hot, yo, and I'm not talking about the weather!"

Cara looked up from pounding her laptop. "I've booked you a fuel stop in Bangkok, Thailand."

"Can we make it that far?" Dan asked anxiously, hanging on to the handle of the portable aquarium with its precious cargo.

"On fumes," the man acknowledged.

"Hey, if it isn't off the chain, the Wiz wants no part of it. Welcome aboard, homeys!"

They filed up the small staircase—Amy, Dan, Jake, Atticus, Hamilton, Jonah, and Ian. Cara stayed behind. It was important for her to rejoin Galt and the family. Her new job would be to serve as the Cahills' agent on Pierce Landing.

Ian lingered on the bottom step, reluctant to part from her. "I'm sorry we doubted you. I of all people should have understood that having a bad parent doesn't necessarily make you bad, too."

"I would have doubted me, too," she said. "It's not easy to get past last names like ours."

Ian marveled at the comment. Kabra and Pierce, two surnames as loaded as hand grenades. This Ekat girl was cleverer than the inventor of the polo-saddle iPhone dock. "You really came through for us, Cara. If I don't see you again—that is, if I don't survive whatever's coming—I want you to know that—" His ordinarily nimble mind let him down, and he announced, "Should I ever be subjected to torture, it will be you I think of as I attempt to hold out."

"How romantic," she told him with an odd grin.

"My point, in actuality—" he blurted. Now he sounded like Atticus Rosenbloom. All he needed was the dreadlocks. This shouldn't be so hard for a *Lucian*—"is, well—you're the greatest."

"*Second* greatest," she amended. "Pony was the

greatest. I'm just a worthy adversary."

"Yes, but what I actually meant was—"

Hamilton reached down from the plane, grabbed Ian by the collar, and hauled him bodily aboard. "Let's go, lover boy. You're holding up the works."

The door closed, and the plane turned around. Ian was at the window to catch a last glimpse of Cara as the jet started back to the runway. She was waving at all of them, but he was positive that her farewell was aimed especially at him.

Jonah bounced his passport off the back of Ian's head. "Seat belt, bro!"

And by the time he could buckle up and look out again, Cara had retreated into the jungle. Right then, Ian knew with absolute certainty that he would never again meet anyone who understood him so completely—who grasped what it meant to be a Kabra or a Pierce.

At that instant, the tower lit up like a Christmas tree, online once more.

Three police SUVs drove over the countryside and bumped onto the tarmac of the landing strip. Sirens wailing, they accelerated fast, closing the gap with the Gulfstream. But they couldn't outrun the power and thrust of jet engines. The G6 burst forward and lifted off into the sky, folding its landing gear beneath it.

In the distance, the lotus spires of Angkor Wat silently watched them go.

PIERCE PROMISES "BIG NEWS"
AT CLAMBAKE

A spokesman for J. Rutherford Pierce has promised a key announcement at the media tycoon's "All-American Clambake" this Sunday, in two days' time. It is widely speculated that this "big news" will be the announcement that Pierce intends to run for president on the Patriotist ticket, a party created by the billionaire himself.

Pierce, who emerged from obscurity to control the world's largest media empire, has taken the political scene by storm. He will enter the presidential race as an instant heavyweight and odds-on favorite to win. The clambake will take place on Pierce Landing, the family's private island off the coast of Maine. The guest list has not been published, but sources say it will include celebrities, former presidents, sports heroes, royalty, Nobel laureates, and at least half of *Forbes*'s list of the wealthiest individuals. Media outlets from thirty-seven different countries will be carrying the event live, and the TV audience is projected to dwarf even the Super Bowl's.

Whatever J. Rutherford Pierce wants to tell us on Sunday, he will have the collective ear of the entire world. . . .

Nellie crumpled up the newspaper clipping and tossed it into the nearest wastebasket. "What an idiot. Who thinks the most all-American thing is clams? Ask the folks in Iowa how many clams they run into in the course of a day."

Sammy was nervous. "This is serious, Nellie. We just blew up this guy's serum factory, and he knows exactly who we are. If he gets to be president, we're going to have to form an expedition to colonize Mars."

The two had traded one lab for another. Now they were in an underground facility below the campus of Harvard University in Cambridge, Massachusetts. It was the lab of Dr. Sylvia Seung, Sammy's mentor and a cousin of the famous Oh family that had once dominated the Ekaterina branch. Although they were no longer prisoners, Sammy and Nellie rarely appeared aboveground in case Pierce's forces were looking for them.

Dr. Seung was surveying a vast mosaic of notes, diagrams, and chemical formulas that covered an entire wall of the lab. "Sammy, is this for real? Who on earth could imagine the chemical properties of the whiskers of an extinct leopard or a crystal formed by a prehistoric meteor strike?"

"It's a long story, Professor," Sammy admitted. "A very old recipe from Olivia Cahill herself. She cobbled it together from the ancient wisdom of the greatest lost civilizations the world has ever known—from Tikal, to Troy, to Angkor. I don't understand exactly how it's going to work yet, but all the ingredients will be coming here. It's up to me to put them together and synthesize more."

The sound of voices in the hall brought Nellie to her feet, quivering with excitement. "They're here! My kiddos are here, safe and sound!"

And then Dan burst in the door and threw himself at her. *"Nellie!"*

She embraced him, then stepped back, surveying him from head to toe. "You're a foot taller! It's been less than a month. What are you eating, Miracle-Gro?"

"Nothing compares with your cooking!" Dan replied, hugging her tightly.

"You would have loved my last creation," Nellie told him with satisfaction. "Nitroglycerin milk shake, extra, extra, extra large. Pierce's lab is still raining down in fine dust."

Dan shook his head with admiration. "Nobody messes with you."

Nellie's attention shifted to Jonah. "Last time I saw

your famous mug, you were trending on YouTube for saving a lunkhead from crocodiles." She turned to Hamilton, giving his massive biceps an affectionate squeeze. "The lunkhead, I presume."

Hamilton smiled sheepishly. "Good to see you, Nellie. Kabra says hi, too."

"Ian? Where is he?"

"He's in quarantine at the airport," Dan supplied, "surrounded by people in hazmat suits. They think he might have a tropical disease."

"Does he?" Nellie asked in concern.

"Nah," Dan explained. "Our snake bit him on the nose, but we couldn't say that without admitting we were smuggling a protected animal out of Cambodia and into the United States. They'll cut him loose when the swelling comes down and the rash goes away."

Nellie laughed. "It's good for a Lucian to take one for the team." Her gaze fell on the last to arrive, Atticus, Jake, and finally Amy.

Nellie had been the Cahill kids' au pair, their protector, and then their legal guardian. She was the closest thing to a parent they'd had since losing their mother and father. So it was with the eyes of love that she looked at Amy and saw the toll the serum had taken on her.

On the surface, Amy was the picture of health—athletic and strong, brimming with energy and glowing with an inner light. But on closer inspection, her robust exterior seemed to hide many troubling details.

She was more muscular, but thinner, with hollow cheeks and deep-set eyes. Her gait and posture were graceful and confident, like that of a star athlete. Yet her smaller movements were shaky, and her hand seemed to have the tremor of a ninety-year-old.

Nellie Gomez was 100 percent tough and ready for anything. She had a tenacity that could be applied equally to perfecting a puff pastry or destroying a billion-dollar lab. But the sight of Amy made her break down and cry.

"It's all good," Jonah soothed, placing a hand on Nellie's shoulder. "We've got the ingredients for the antidote." He nodded in Sammy's direction. "What up, genius? Ready to do your thing?"

"I'll try," Sammy promised nervously.

He sounded far less certain than they would have hoped for with Amy's life — and the fate of the planet — hanging in the balance.

Amy deftly applied pressure with her thumb to the head of the Tonle Sap water snake. The small fangs came down, piercing the thick latex that covered the beaker. The Cahills watched as clear droplets of venom pearled on the fangs and splashed into the container.

Jonah was bug-eyed. "That's it? The Wiz was almost croc chow for *that*?"

Amy massaged the venom glands to make sure there

was no more liquid to be had. "I hope it's enough," she said anxiously.

Sammy measured carefully. "We only need a tiny batch. Then we can analyze the molecular composition and synthesize a large quantity."

Next the Anatolian leopard whiskers were ground to powder and suspended in solution. The riven crystal was melted to a liquid state. One by one, the ingredients were meticulously prepared and measured.

While Sammy worked his magic in the lab, Dr. Seung, who was also an MD, gave Amy a thorough physical exam. The results were all over the place. She registered astounding strength and record-setting reflexes. However, Amy's heart was racing to keep pace with a metabolic rate that medical science had never seen. She scored off the charts on vision and hearing tests, but her blood pressure was so high that the cuff blew right off her arm. An EEG revealed brainwaves on a par with the greatest minds in history, yet her tremors were consistent with a patient in the advanced stages of Parkinson's disease. There was no speed on the treadmill that she could not maintain comfortably. Although she showed no symptoms of fever, her body temperature was approaching 105.

Eventually, all the doctor-speak became too much for Dan. "Cut the mumbo-jumbo, doc. Give it to us straight. One minute she's too sick; the next she's too well."

"She's both," Dr. Seung explained. "In order to perform at this extraordinary level, her body is literally burning itself out."

Jake's voice was barely a whisper. "How long?"

"If I had to guess—and I do," Dr. Seung replied, "I'd say two days, maybe less."

Now Dan's own heart was pounding, no serum required. *It's happening! It's really happening! Amy's dying!*

Amy nodded stoically. "It adds up. The estimate was always about a week, and I took the serum five days ago."

"Adds up!" Jake's stress bubbled over. "Amy, how can you talk so clinically about your *life*! If the snake hadn't climbed into Ian's shoe, we'd still be in Cambodia, looking! We could easily have missed our one chance to save you!"

"But we *didn't*," Amy reminded him.

"Yeah, by sheer random chance!"

Amy and Dan shared a flash of the almost tele-pathic connection that had grown between them since the loss of their parents. Brilliant as he was, Jake was not a Cahill, and he couldn't possibly understand the lesson they'd learned in the search for the 39 Clues. There was no point worrying about what might have happened. As long as you were still alive, still in the hunt, that was a good day. There was antidote to be made and a presidential wannabe to be foiled. That was all that mattered.

Amy and Dan lived in the moment, because hard experience had taught them that there was no other time.

Ian was finally released by US immigration close to midnight. By the time he made it to the lab, the place was deserted. It took twenty minutes of pounding against a heavy steel door to wake an exhausted Sammy, who had fallen asleep at his worktable.

"Where is everyone?" Ian asked in irritation.

"Dr. Seung got them apartments in a residence for visiting professors," Sammy replied. "It's the middle of the night, Ian."

Ian nodded. "How lovely to know that they were comfortable while I was poked and prodded and drained of half my blood so the Center for Disease Control could test for the Ebola virus."

The big news was that the antidote had been created, analyzed, and synthesized. It was ready for testing.

Ian forgot his grievances and sprinted out of the building to rally the Cahill troops.

Soon the entire group was back in the lab, gathered around a single hypodermic syringe filled with an opaque milky liquid. They looked at it with reverence.

Atticus was the first to put the emotion into words. "I know it's just a dose of gray slime and all, but think where it comes from—and who! The wisdom of lost civilizations, collected by Leonardo da Vinci himself!"

"And his lab assistant, Olivia Cahill," put in Dan. "It was her notebook that made this even possible."

"This is like a life-saving gift handed down through the centuries from the mother of our family," Amy added in a hushed tone.

"It's all that," Jonah agreed.

"I prepared it as a shot because that's the fastest way to deliver it to the bloodstream," Sammy explained. "But it could also be taken by mouth or even converted to an aerosol spray."

"Faster is definitely better," Nellie decided. She turned to Amy. "Kiddo, roll up your sleeve."

Amy's reply was a single word. "No."

Instantly, she had everyone's attention. "Quit fooling around," Dan growled at her. "You need the antidote."

"And I'll take it," she promised, "but not yet."

"When?" Jake blurted. "Tomorrow? The day after? You don't know if you have that much time!"

Amy squeezed her eyes shut to force away the pinwheels of color that were swirling all around her. Her hallucinations were becoming more frequent and intense, as were the tremors, but at least now there was light at the end of the tunnel. Their long, meandering journey through the capitals of antiquity had a scheduled ending—Sunday, at the All-American

FLASHPOINT

Clambake on Pierce Landing. The antidote would save her life, but it would also take away her biggest advantage going into that final battle. How could she place her own well-being above the future of the world?

"Once Pierce announces he's running for president," Amy tried to explain, "he'll have Secret Service protection and platoons of journalists following him everywhere he goes. We won't be able to get near him. That makes the clambake our last chance to derail his freight train. To pull this off, I need to be the way I am now—stronger, faster, and smarter."

Nellie lifted several inches off the floor. "You might not be stronger, faster, and smarter *then*! You might not even be alive!"

"It's a risk," Amy admitted. "But the plain truth is there's no other way. Pierce is enhanced; so are Galt and the family's whole army of minions and goons. We need that boost on our side, too."

"Why?" Dan shot back in anguish. "We kept up with those idiots before you took the serum."

"Well, for starters, we need a way to get the antidote to Pierce Landing. Right now I can learn how to fly a plane in a matter of hours."

Nellie jumped in. "I'm a pilot. I can fly the plane!"

"But on the serum, I'll be more than a pilot," Amy argued. "I'll be a one-person command center."

"Maybe you won't need to," Nellie argued bitterly. "Maybe the plan will go perfectly and you'll end up tossing your life away for nothing!"

"Maybe," Amy conceded. "But that doesn't change anything."

"Forget it." Jake played his trump card. "You put Dan in charge, and there's no way he's going to go for it." He looked to Dan for confirmation.

The answer was a long time coming. Dan thought hard, his expression torn. "I'm with Amy," he said finally. "This thing is too important. It's like Luke Skywalker trying to destroy the Death Star. We've got one shot, and if we blow it, the whole galaxy pays the price."

The argument ceased. The group had learned through hard experience that some missions took absolutely priority. There were things that had to be gotten exactly right, or nothing else would matter.

Dan swallowed hard. At least 40 percent of him had been cheering for the others to shout him down. He could not see the future, but one thing seemed absolutely crystal clear: If Amy died because of this decision, he would never be able to live with himself.

The sheer weight of it threatened to crush him into the floor, almost as if the force of gravity had been tripled through some fiat of nature. All he wanted was to be free of the Cahills, yet here he was—not merely involved, but calling the shots, with nothing less than Amy's life on the line. Decisions had to be made, and he was the one who had to make them. For that alone, he felt a blinding hatred toward J. Rutherford Pierce he'd never believed himself capable of.

He realized that he would never get away from all this Cahill craziness — not alone anyway. The only way out would be with Amy at his side. If she survived the next twenty-four hours — if they both did — they would quit the family together.

"Can I ask a practical question?" Sammy broke the solemn silence. "If Amy's not going to test the antidote, who is? I mean, *someone* has to. All this is for nothing if the antidote doesn't work."

Hamilton had a suggestion. "We could always test it out on one of Pierce's souped-up goons."

Amy shook her head. "No good. Pierce's people know us too well. The last thing we want is to tip them off that we've completed the antidote."

"What about Cara?" Jonah suggested. "Nobody would ever suspect her."

Ian shook his head. "She's already on Pierce Landing. By the time we could get her some antidote to test, it would be too late to change our plans."

Atticus spoke up bravely. "I volunteer to take the serum. Then you could try the antidote on me."

"Don't even think about it!" snapped Jake, drawing his little brother close.

Dan regarded his best friend in genuine affection and respect. "You rock, buddy. But we'd never allow you to do something like that. And nobody else, either."

Nellie had an idea. "Well, there is one person. . . ."

CHAPTER 21

As the taxi from LaGuardia Airport drove Nellie through the streets of New York, she passed her favorite French bakery and knew a moment of yearning and regret. It was still far from sunrise, and people were already queued up at Au Delice, home of the flakiest, most exquisite croissants outside of France. It took all her willpower to keep from jumping out of the cab and getting in line. Alas, this was the Cahill world. The delights of life were all around you — right under your nose sometimes. But no, you had to take care of business, because business was usually life and death.

Her destination was not too far away, on Manhattan's Upper East Side — the Callender Institute. She noted that the flag was at half mast, no doubt to mark the passing of their founder, Dr. Jeffrey Callender. Nellie was surprised at the wave of regret that came over her. If anybody deserved his fate, it was Callender — a staunch Pierce ally who was using Fiske Cahill as a human guinea pig. Yet as much as Nellie had wanted to destroy the Delaware lab and everything in it, she and Sammy had worked so hard to protect the *people* — to make sure that the staff got out before the nitroglycerin explosions began their march down Kablooey Avenue. They had succeeded in every case except one. She still found it in her heart to regret the death of Jeffrey Callender.

On the other hand, it was just as well that the doctor wasn't there to try to prevent her from seeing Fiske.

The receptionist smiled at Nellie without suspicion. "Welcome back, but I'm afraid you're a little early. Visiting hours don't begin until noon."

Undaunted, Nellie delivered a long rambling speech about having just gotten off the plane from Europe, and, oh, how she longed to see her dear uncle. She was so emotional, so noisy, and so persistent that the young woman let her through "just this once."

Nellie took the elevator to Fiske's floor and started down the corridor, steering clear of anyone in a lab coat. Most of the staff were regular medical personnel, but a few of the male "nurses" were unusually broad and muscular and bore a troubling resemblance to Pierce's goons. She proceeded cautiously, marveling at the luxury of the plush carpet, oak paneling, and recessed halogen lighting. It was pretty posh for a medical facility — the institute was known to cater to the wealthy. She felt a stab of anger. Not only was poor Fiske being experimented on, but he was paying through the nose for the privilege.

And then she was peering in the doorway at him.

He was sitting up in bed, reading the paper—at least, that *seemed* to be his plan. In fact, he was staring listlessly at the wall while the *New York Times* drooped in his hands. He looked awful—much worse than the last time she'd seen him. True, he showed a few traces of the enhancement that could be found in Amy or J. Rutherford Pierce. His face had that healthy glow, but his eyes and cheeks were hollow. His flesh hung off his bones, as if he were a former star athlete who hadn't exercised in decades. Horribly, he reminded Nellie of the skeleton figure on the tarot card Death. With a pang, she noted that the hands that held the newspaper were trembling.

"It's good to see you, Fiske." It was half a lie. Yes, it was good to see him, but it was terrible to see him like this.

"Nellie!" He was absurdly happy to welcome her, which showed how lonely and miserable he'd been.

She hugged him, and couldn't get over the feeling that she was embracing a burlap sack filled with Lincoln Logs. "I'm sorry no one's been able to visit. We've all been—busy."

He gave her a warm smile. "I know what that's about. Remember, my name is Cahill." The smile wavered. "And yet, since you last came here, I seem to have become—old."

"No way," she told him firmly.

"I'm not a child, Nellie. Sooner or later, everybody comes to the end of the road." His voice cracked a little.

"I do confess, however, that my exit seems to have arrived rather—unexpectedly. And now, just when I need him most, my doctor has succumbed to a tragic accident."

Nellie leaned closer. "Listen to me, Fiske. You're not dying."

"That's very kind of you, dear, but—"

"I'm not being kind," she insisted, "I'm telling you the truth. There's nothing wrong with you except that your sweet, sainted doctor was working for Pierce. He's been experimenting on you with Gideon's serum."

"Interesting," the old man said, wide-eyed. "Is that why I feel like I can leap tall buildings, when in reality I can barely walk across this room?"

She nodded. "We all know what that stuff does to people."

"Thank you, Nellie, for letting me know exactly what's been happening to me. It puts my mind at rest, although it can do nothing to change the outcome of all this. For what Gideon created there is no cure. Hard cheese for me, unfortunately."

Nellie took a small case from her pocketbook and removed a carefully wrapped syringe. "This is the antidote. It's untested, but it comes straight from Olivia Cahill's notebook."

Fiske was amazed. "How did you get it?"

"It was a family affair. Cahills collected the ingredients from all over the world—mostly Amy and Dan. They're amazing. I'll give you the whole story later.

But right now I have to ask you to be a guinea pig again—for a good cause this time. Can we test the antidote on you?"

The old man was already rolling up his sleeve. "Even if it's deadly poison, I'd be no worse off than I already am. Let's have it!"

Nellie had to clench her teeth to keep them from chattering as she injected the opaque liquid. One person was already dead as a result of her actions. If it happened to Fiske . . .

"How do you feel?" she asked anxiously.

"I feel—I feel—" Suddenly, Fiske twisted in agony, a raspy rattle issuing from his throat. An instant later, his eyes rolled back in his head and he collapsed against his pillows.

Panicked, Nellie took hold of his shoulders and shook him. "Fiske—wake up! Don't do this to me!" She reached for the call button to the nursing station, wondering what on earth she could possibly tell them—that he was having an allergic reaction to Anatolian leopard whiskers and the slightly poisonous venom of the Tonle Sap water snake?

A hand reached up and grabbed her arm—a surprisingly strong hand.

"No need, my dear. I'm going to be just fine."

CHAPTER 22

Amy worked the controls with the confidence and ease of a seasoned pilot.

In the monitoring booth, the supervisor watched her video feed. "No way that girl hasn't flown before," he said to Jake, who was fidgeting uncomfortably in the chair beside him. "She's an ace!"

The flight simulator was located on the campus of the Massachusetts Institute of Technology, and the instructor was a former Navy Top Gun. The man never would have bothered with a novice pilot, and a civilian at that. But Admiral McAllister owed Eisenhower Holt—Hamilton's father—a favor. The Cahills, Jake reflected, seemed to be owed an endless amount of favors all around the world.

Through the glass, the simulator tilted forward and righted itself as Amy put her "aircraft" into a dive and then leveled off. The Top Gun whistled with admiration. "Outstanding! I know test pilots who couldn't match your girlfriend's scores!"

Jake winced. Every word of praise fell on him like a

hammer blow. He'd been hoping that Amy would wash out at this, so she could take the antidote right away and let Nellie do the flying.

"She's not my girlfriend," he mumbled aloud.

"Yeah, right. I've seen the way you two look at each other." The man spoke into the comm microphone. "Doing fine. Now bank to the left and take it to five thousand feet. Over."

"Roger that." Amy performed the maneuver flawlessly.

Jake looked on bleakly. She'd never agree to the shot now. The serum was making her too good.

The instructor regarded him in amazement. "What's your problem? She's killing it, and you've got a face like your dog just died."

"I've got to get out of here," Jake moaned. "Is there someplace I could get a cup of coffee?"

"Cafeteria's down the hall to your left. Pick me up an iced tea, will you?"

Once in the corridor, Jake crumpled against the wall. He used to think that nothing could be worse than witnessing Amy's deterioration with no antidote in sight.

Now the antidote was more than in sight — it was in their hands! And still Amy refused it.

He'd been wrong before. *This* was worse.

The supervisor watched Jake out the door, then turned back to his monitor. The girl was so focused and in control that he was barely paying attention now. But what he saw next made him sit bolt upright. Amy's eyes rolled back in her head. Her body stiffened, her hands still gripping the wheel, her arms shaking.

The Top Gun was not a doctor and could not have explained what was happening to her. One thing, however, was obvious to him. If she'd been flying a real plane and not a simulator, the result would have been an engine stall, a steep nosedive, a fiery explosion, and a search for the black box flight recorder to figure out what had gone wrong.

He hit the ABORT button and raced up the ramp to the simulator. The door had opened automatically, providing a view of Amy slumped over the controls. He eased her back in the seat and slapped gently at her pale cheeks.

"Okay, kid. Come back. You're all right."

Amy's eyelids fluttered open. "What—?"

"You tell me. You passed out and then you crashed."

She frowned. "Jake—the guy I came with—did he see?"

The man shook his head. "He went out for coffee."

She set her jaw. "He cannot find out. Not a word, okay?"

"Not my business," he agreed. "But you shouldn't fly, or even take lessons. Not until a doctor clears you first. You can't take the risk that what happened today will happen when you're really up there. Understand?"

She nodded, understanding perfectly. The Top Gun was not a Cahill. Which meant he didn't even know the meaning of the word *risk*.

Dan felt his ears pop as the high-speed elevator bore him up to the thirty-seventh floor, where Aunt Beatrice lived in a luxury penthouse.

Figures, he thought in disgust. *When she was our guardian, she kept us low-rent, dumped off on a series of au pairs.* He smiled. He couldn't regret that part, since it had brought Nellie into their lives.

The marble décor of the hallway reminded Dan of Rome, only newer, and with fresh flowers everywhere. The Cahills had plenty of money to go around, but Dan found himself resenting that his great-aunt — who did jack squat for the family — was sharing so generously in it.

Another resident gave him a dirty look as they passed in the corridor, the man's nose twitching. *Probably doesn't like kids*, Dan reflected before remembering that the package he was carrying most likely didn't smell so great. He was already half sorry he'd come here, and he hadn't even knocked on the door yet.

And then there she was, ancient Aunt Beatrice, in her mid-eighties now. She stepped back to allow him to enter, presenting her wrinkled, rouged cheek to be kissed. In some ways, she resembled her younger sister, Dan's grandmother, Grace, but minus the lively intelligence and good humor. Grace's eyes had been twin sparklers on the Fourth of July, her smile utterly captivating. Aunt Beatrice's eyes looked like two stewed prunes, and she never smiled at all.

"You haven't grown much," the old lady observed, as if he had stayed short on purpose.

"Nice to see you, too," Dan replied, peering around the palatial apartment in search of the one he had really come to visit.

At last, he received the greeting he'd been waiting for. A silver Egyptian Mau wandered out of the kitchen, tail in the air. *"Mrrrp."*

"Saladin!" Dan was overjoyed to see Grace's cat — technically, Amy and Dan's cat by inheritance. Saladin trotted over and presented his noble head to be scratched.

Dan began to unwrap his parcel. "I brought you some fresh snapper. Quincy Market — the good stuff."

At the smell of fish, Saladin rubbed up against Dan's jeans, nudging him in the direction of the kitchen and his food bowl.

"Your cat has been horrible, by the way," Aunt Beatrice called from the living room. "His infernal purring keeps me up all night, and don't get me started on that awful litter box."

"Do you change it every week?" Dan asked.

"Of course not. That's why I choose not to keep

animals in the apartment—so I won't have to deal with such malodorous things. I simply don't understand why you and your sister can't take him!"

Dan had a vision of poor Saladin scrambling for his life with a Cambodian crocodile in pursuit. "Grace would have wanted it this way."

He was laying out the snapper when he heard another voice. This one belonged to the last person he expected to encounter in a Cahill home.

"The whole trouble with the United Nations is there are too many foreigners!"

Dan's head snapped up. "Pierce?" he exclaimed in bewilderment.

Through the kitchen doorway, he could see the TV tuned to CNN—Pierce, onstage, haranguing a worshipful crowd.

"It's his last big speech before the clambake," Aunt Beatrice enthused. "I swear, if I were a younger woman, I'd go to Pierce Landing to show my support in person."

Didn't it figure? She was a Piercer.

"Look at dear Debi Ann," the old lady went on, brimming with admiration. "Always by his side, so loyal. What a perfect first lady she'll make. She's a cousin, you know."

"I've met her kids," Dan commented. "Human-being-wise, she's one for two."

Aunt Beatrice wasn't even listening. "They have a perfect marriage. I'm so glad Rutherford found Debi Ann after that silly infatuation with Hope."

"Hope?" Dan choked. The mere mention of Mom's name clutched right at his heart. "You mean Mom? She used to date *Pierce*?" He shuddered, unwilling to let his vision of Pierce tarnish the tiny shards of memory he carried of his mother.

"He was in love with her, poor man. But she only had eyes for that awful Arthur Trent."

Dan glared at her. "That 'awful Arthur Trent' was my father."

"Hope was so headstrong—like her mother," the old lady rambled on. "She was too flighty to appreciate a sterling character like Rutherford."

All at once, Dan decided he'd had all he could take of his great-aunt's company. "I guess I'd better get going. Nice to see you, Aunt Beatrice. Peace out, Saladin."

"It was wonderful of you to come," the old lady replied formally, as if speaking to a stranger. "You've always been a good boy deep down. Such a pity that your sister doesn't share your sense of responsibility."

Dan saw red. "Don't say that!" How dare this woman who had as much warmth and humanity as Saladin's fresh fish dump all over Amy, who was taking the troubles of the entire world onto her shoulders? "Amy's got more sense of responsibility than anybody I know! She's devoted her whole life to this family, the same way Grace always did, maybe even more! She didn't come with me because she *couldn't*! She's sick—" His voice broke. *"Really* sick."

For the first time, his great-aunt seemed genuinely moved. "What's wrong with her?"

Dan was on the verge of tears. He was holding it together dealing with Amy's situation. But having to talk about it was almost more than he could handle. "It's—a rare condition—"

"Bring her to me," the old woman insisted. "I'll take her to my personal physician."

"I—I gotta go!" He fled, taking the stairs for all thirty-six flights so his elderly aunt couldn't follow him.

From the mansion on Pierce Landing, the distant Maine coast was nothing but a thin strip of purple capping the endless Atlantic blue.

Cara slipped out of her parents' home and stood on the stone patio watching the glow of the sun just beneath the horizon. A lighthouse winked.

"America," came a voice behind her. "Starting tomorrow, it's going to be ours."

Her father came out to join her, placing an arm around her shoulders.

She laughed. "You're not invading it; you're running for president."

"Same difference," he told her. "Everything you do in this life, every undertaking, every goal you set yourself is a kind of battle. And you can win or lose. Never forget that, Cara. No matter how great your position, losing is always a possibility."

"*You* never lose."

"Once," he admitted, his eyes clouding at the memory of Hope Cahill. "But that was a long time ago. And I want you to know that the presidency is just the beginning. One day, we Pierces will take our place at the head of a family of nations never before seen on this planet. I've made it our destiny."

"One thing at a time. Right, Dad?"

He beamed at her. "Forever practical. I need someone like you—someone who understands that every grand design must be implemented one step at a time. I've been watching you these past weeks."

She tensed for a moment. Watching her? What had he seen? What did he know?

"It's always been understood that your brother would succeed me, but lately I've been wondering if he has the stuff. There's a lot of Mom in him. We don't need more teddy bears; we need moxie! The way he gummed things up in Cambodia—"

"Those Cahills are not to be underestimated," she offered in defense of Galt. Cara knew her brother couldn't stand her, and the feeling was pretty much mutual. But it was hard to grow up in the shadow of a bombastic dynamo—and harder still for Galt, who had once been Dad's fair-haired boy, and now seemed to have lost that most-favored status.

"I know," Pierce sighed. "I remember their mother. But you—you're a true Pierce. Don't go waltzing off with some handsome young man, because I've got a big future in mind for you." The sun slipped behind the strip of mainland, leaving them in dusk. "It may look peaceful now, but just wait till tomorrow. Boats, helicopters — the joint's going to be jumping. Everybody who's anybody will be coming right here. This little island will be the center of the universe."

She experienced a flicker of regret. He was still her father. And in his own way, he loved her. "You really think you can win? The presidency, I mean?"

He flashed her an enigmatic grin. "Big things come in small packages."

Something about the way he said it worried her. It was mischievous, but also ominous — the tone of a prankster whose prank is something truly terrible.

She tried to conceal her misgivings in order to draw him out. "Our next president talks in riddles, Dad?" she chided.

"Big things come in small packages," he repeated. "And I've got six, hidden all around the globe. Don't worry, you'll know soon enough. The whole world will know soon enough."

Her father would not reveal his twisted plan, whatever it was.

Cara set her jaw. He was right about one thing, though. She was a true Pierce. And Pierces didn't hesitate to do what needed to be done.

CHAPTER 23

The Zodiac inflatable raft cut through the choppy waves at high speed, shaking the four occupants like rag dolls and drenching them with cold water.

"I'm going to puke," Dan threatened in the darkness.

"Such a lovely word," Ian commented miserably. "Have you considered something more civilized, like 'throw up' or perhaps 'give back'?"

"In my hood, they call it 'tossing a sidewalk pizza,'" Jonah managed.

"Your 'hood'?" Hamilton echoed from his place at the wheel. "You live in a row of twenty-million-dollar palaces. Do you even *have* sidewalks?"

They had left the coast of Maine just after midnight, navigating via GPS in near-total blackness. A wind had come up early on, and the ocean was rough and inhospitable.

"You think we missed it, yo?" Jonah worried. "It's mad small, right?"

"According to the GPS, it's dead ahead," Hamilton insisted.

Ian took out his phone, cupping his hands around it to protect it from the spray. "Cara, are you there? We can't find the island."

"It's right here where it always is," her voice crackled in reply. "Oh, look, the swelling has gone down on your nose. You're almost cute again."

"Cut it out," Dan snapped. "This isn't a pleasure cruise. We're tossing pizzas here. Can't you turn on a light or something?"

"No can do," came the reply. "This place is crawling with security. Give me a second to put on my night-vision goggles. . . . Wait, I see you. Make a twenty-degree correction to port."

It wasn't easy to navigate blind, but with Cara's detailed directions, Hamilton managed to pilot the small craft to the island's craggy coast. The newcomers splashed ashore, grateful to be on dry land.

"I'd kiss the ground, but I don't think I'd have the strength to straighten up again," groaned Dan.

"Shhh," Cara cautioned. "My dad brought in every serum-juiced piece of hired muscle on the payroll."

"Exactly how many goons are we talking about?" Ian asked. "We Lucians like to know exactly what we're up against."

"There must be at least a hundred of them."

A hush fell as the Cahills absorbed these hideous odds. Not only were they behind enemy lines, but they were horribly outnumbered.

"No way to beat them in a fair fight," Hamilton

observed. "Or even an unfair one."

"Your father made one strategic error, though," Ian mused. "He put all his eggs in one basket. The sum total of his assets is on Pierce Landing. That makes him vulnerable."

"If Amy and Jake can deliver the payload, yo," added Jonah nervously.

"They'd better," Dan breathed, "or we're going to be left hanging like prime rib in a shark tank."

The five deflated the Zodiac and buried it completely under rocks and bushes. With the sun rising on clambake day, there must be no sign that Pierce Landing had any uninvited guests. Staying low, the group followed Cara over the dark terrain. Keeping them away from any patrols or security cameras, she brought them to a remote equipment shed well concealed by trees. In the moonlight, they could make out the hulking silhouette of the main house half a mile away.

She produced a key and opened the hut door. "You should be safe here. There are four sets of coveralls—the same kind the maintenance staff wears. Also hats and sunglasses to hide your faces. Once the crowds start to arrive, I'll come back and sneak you into the stage area. That's where the big announcement will be made."

They entered the small structure, which was piled high with gardening equipment.

"Not a ton of space for a big guy," Hamilton noted,

settling his broad beam on a stack of fertilizer bags. He pulled a folded tarp off a wheelbarrow. "Jackpot!"

A full picnic had been laid out on a clean cloth, complete with sandwiches, chips, energy bars, and drinks.

"I figured you'd need to keep your strength up," Cara supplied.

"That's very thoughtful, Cara," Ian said wanly. "The only thing missing would be the perfect cup of tea to go with it."

She reached inside a watering can and pulled out a tall silver thermos. "Earl Grey, milk, two lumps."

Ian Kabra had found the girl of his dreams. He would not let her get away — *if* he survived the next twelve hours.

Mr. and Mrs. Floyd Penobscot of Saco, Maine, had never before won anything in their lives. That was why they were amazed when the notification came from the Jelly of the Month Club that their names had been selected for the grand prize in the annual Jam-stakes — a week-long Caribbean cruise, all expenses paid.

One puzzling note — neither husband nor wife could recall having entered the annual Jam-stakes. But the couple wasn't going to argue with a free vacation, airfare included. Arm in arm, they boarded the plane, filled with anticipation of the adventure to come.

As soon as Flight 5537 took off from Portland,

a notification from the airline pinged on Atticus Rosenbloom's cell phone. "The Penobscots are on their way," he reported. "This is a real thing, right? I mean, we didn't just send those poor people all the way to Florida only to find out there's no cruise."

The comment drew a short chuckle from Amy, and that was really saying something. She could not have imagined herself capable of any kind of laughter in her current state — shivering one moment, sweating the next, seeing things that weren't there, her field of vision a Technicolor lightning storm. And always those tremors.

"Don't worry," she soothed Atticus, "the cruise is real even if the contest wasn't. I booked them a first-class cabin, panoramic terrace, dinner at the captain's table. The Penobscots are going in style."

Sammy turned the key in the ignition, and the big rented cube van coughed back to life. Sammy, Amy, and the Rosenblooms had spent the last two hours parked on the shoulder of County Road 5 waiting for word that the prizewinners were on their way. The truck crunched onto the pavement and drove the last few miles to the Penobscot property outside Saco. There was a neat wood-frame house set well back from the road, but the main feature was a small airstrip. The sign by the front mailbox read PENOBSCOT AGRICUL-TURAL AVIATION. Underneath that was a single word that explained it all: CROP DUSTING.

Sammy guided the truck up the long drive, past the

house, and out to the airstrip. A white-painted Quonset hut sat next to the tarmac, sheltering a faded single-engine biplane with a fat body and the name *Roslyn* painted on the side.

"Whoa!" Atticus exclaimed. "Didn't the Red Baron refuse to fly one of these because it was too old?"

"All it has to do is get high enough off the ground to spray crops, Att," Jake told his brother. "We don't need a stealth bomber."

"Pierce Landing is less than thirty miles from the coast," Amy added. "A crop-dusting business services customers who are farther away than that."

Amy kicked away the blocks, and the four of them were able to roll the Grumman aircraft out of the hangar. The crop duster itself was extremely light; most of its weight came from fuel and the contents of its huge spray tanks. These were normally filled with pesticides. For today's mission, however, the Cahills had a different cargo in mind.

Sammy raised the truck's rear door to reveal an enormous stainless steel container. He unrolled the connected hose and inserted the nozzle into the plane's payload tank. A switch on the container started the pumping action. A clattering noise and the sloshing of liquid had them shouting to be heard.

"Did you know it was going to be this loud?" Jake complained. "I really don't feel like explaining to some nosy neighbor why we're pumping seven hundred gallons of antidote into a crop duster!"

Amy shrugged. "You know the cover story. We're helping Sammy, who's flying the plane for the Penobscots while they're away."

"This'll take at least an hour," Sammy informed them. "So we'd better get used to it."

Atticus was worried. "This antidote is different than the one Nellie gave Fiske, isn't it?"

Sammy shook his head. "The chemical composition is identical. The only difference is it'll be coming out as a spray instead of an injection. It has to blanket the entire island so that everybody there breathes in enough of the particles to get the full effect. It's the only way we can dose Pierce and all his goons at the same time."

It sounded so reasonable when Sammy said it, but they understood that an awful lot of things would have to go right for this plan to have any chance of success: the aerosolized antidote had to work; the wind couldn't be too strong; the inexperienced pilot had to bring the crop duster in low and at exactly the right moment; Pierce and his people had to be outdoors where the airborne particles would reach them; Dan, Ian, Hamilton, and Jonah had to avoid being detected; Cara could not change sides again and betray them to her father. And the whole operation depended on Amy, who had been on the serum for a week.

Her life — and the success of the mission — were hanging by the same thread.

CHAPTER 24

In the hours that followed sunrise, the population of the tiny island doubled seven times over.

Private jets and helicopters circled the airstrip, awaiting clearance to land. Floatplanes set down on the sparkling water all around Pierce Landing. Their pilots had to be careful, because the ocean teemed with boats ranging from tiny dories and sloops to the luxury yachts of the super-rich. A huge ferry rented from the state of Massachusetts carried more than fifteen hundred ardent Piercers determined to be there in person to see the first-ever Patriotist candidate make his big announcement.

A village of satellite dishes sprouted like mushrooms on the rolling, manicured lawns. The jockeying for the best vantage point to film the day's events was intense. Already, a major network anchor had to be led to the first-aid tent with a bloody nose. The BBC jostled with the Germans, and nobody wanted to be close to the bloggers, who were considered too opinionated. An orbiting communications satellite had been rented exclusively to carry video from Pierce Landing.

Newspaper reporters and TV camerapeople swarmed around the VIP tent, where a Who's Who of celebrities, politicians, business titans, royalty, elite athletes, and entertainers grew longer by the hour.

For a reporter, it was more than just a chance to crown the next political superstar, who would almost certainly go on to become the leader of the free world. Never before had so many of the planet's rich, powerful, and famous gathered in the same place at the same time. It was a once-in-a-lifetime opportunity for interviews.

One reporter's day's work had begun before all the others. His news outlet was small — an online magazine specializing in arts and crafts. But Debi Ann Pierce had been eager to grant him an audience to discuss her homemade teddy bears.

"A teddy bear is so much more than a toy, an inanimate object." The future first lady was in her glory, speaking about her very favorite subject. "It gives us companionship and affection. It gives us *love*."

The reporter was recording her on his cell phone when the device was ripped from his hand. He looked up to see one of the island's burly security men glaring down at him. "Nobody's supposed to be in the main house."

"*I* invited him," Debi Ann spoke up. "It's not a

political interview; he's interested in me and my work."

The suited man was polite but adamant. "You must have forgotten, ma'am. No reporters in the mansion. That comes from the top."

"I'm sure my husband didn't mean me," she insisted.

But her protests fell on deaf ears. The online magazine would have to get by with half a teddy bear interview. As the man was escorted out of the house, Debi Ann went looking for her husband.

She found him alone in the study, rehearsing his speech in front of a mirror.

"Rutherford, why did you stop my interview?"

Pierce's eyes never left his own reflection. "Rules are rules, Debi Ann."

"I thought you said you're the one who makes the rules. That interview made me feel good about myself and my teddy bears."

He turned to face her, suppressing a tremor in his arm. "Did it ever occur to you that I don't want the American people to find out that their next first lady is a one-woman Build-A-Bear Workshop?"

"All first ladies have their special projects," she argued.

"Sure," he retorted sarcastically. "Nutrition. Literacy. Not sewing up a battalion of lopsided, cross-eyed fuzz balls. If Martha Washington had tried something like this, George would have bitten her with his wooden teeth! Why couldn't I have a wife more like—"

She stared at him. "Like *Martha Washington*?" The

guilty look in his eye gave him away. "You're still thinking about Hope Cahill!"

He didn't deny it. Lies came easily to J. Rutherford
Pierce, but not today, the most important day of his life.

"Maybe I was thinking," he said stiffly, his jaw
clenched, "of Letitia Tyler." He brushed past her and
disappeared down the hall.

Debi Ann was bewildered. Why Letitia Tyler?

All at once, she remembered her presidential history. Letitia Christian Tyler died in 1842, while her
husband, John Tyler, was still in office.

A frosty cold began in Debi Ann's extremities and
worked its way into her core. She might enter the White
House on her triumphant husband's arm, but she
would leave in a funeral procession.

Her husband was planning to kill her.

The four boys could hear activity all around
them—muffled conversation, motor noises, shouted
instructions, distant boat horns, PA announcements.

It was driving Dan insane. "I can't handle this," he
murmured. "For all we know, Galt and half the goon
army have surrounded the shed and are about to kick
in the door and kill us. But we can't even peek outside
for fear of giving ourselves away."

The others shared his frustration. "Where's your
girlfriend, Kabra?" Hamilton demanded in an irritated

whisper. "She said she was coming to get us."

"She said she was coming, but not *when*," Ian defended Cara. "We have to assume she's waiting for the right time to sneak us out of here."

"And what if Pierce bugs over a dandelion and sends someone for a weed-whacker?" Jonah challenged.

Ian rolled his eyes. "We can't see what's going on out there. Cara can. She's the one in a position to assess the situation. Honestly, discussing strategy with non-Lucians can be exhausting."

The four were dressed in the blue coveralls and work boots of the island maintenance staff. Jonah added a small false mustache to help conceal his famous features. All understood that the operation that lay ahead would be unthinkably delicate. Anything less than pinpoint timing and execution would result in failure. The danger was so intense that they could almost pull chunks of it out of the air and grasp it in their hands — danger not just for them but for the entire world. If they couldn't stop Pierce here and now, they'd never get another chance. He'd be an official presidential candidate, with Secret Service protection and a media swarm that amounted to an electronic eye on everything that happened within fifty yards of him. Barring a miracle, he'd win the election in a landslide, and then he'd have the entire US military at his command. His dream of global domination would be within reach.

The four exchanged nervous glances. They were

Cahills — up to the challenge, willing to take the risks. But the sitting around was killing them.

"I've got to start touring again, yo," Jonah muttered. "Fans chew you up and spit you out, but this saving the world gig is brutal."

"It could be worse," Dan reminded him in a harsh tone. "My sister is about to fly a plane using arms and legs that don't always work and a brain that could check out at any minute."

The group was silent as his words sank in.

There was a light knocking sound outside the shed. A shaft of brilliant sunlight assailed them as the door opened a crack. They heard Cara's low voice: "It's time."

The boys emerged to find themselves in a very different place than the peaceful island they'd landed on that morning. Crowds surged all around them. It was like a vast carnival, only instead of booths and games, there were mobile units from TV networks — hundreds of them — a jungle of cables, booms, satellite dishes, and cameras. Reporters spoke urgently into microphones.

Cara had chosen the moment well. In all the comings and goings, no one paid any attention to the four newcomers. They disappeared immediately into a work force that blanketed Pierce Landing — hanging bunting, raising flags, and preparing for the balloon drop to follow the big announcement.

People surged in every direction, but the general movement was toward the beach. In freshly dug pits in the sand, wood was stacked for the bonfires, and giant cooking vessels awaited the main course. In the kitchen of the mansion, more than one hundred thousand clams were being prepared for steaming — the largest number in history, according to the *Guinness Book of World Records*.

The stage was a megalith of stars, stripes, and patriotic color. Hamilton nudged Jonah. "Think there's enough red, white, and blue around here?"

The speakers' platform was framed by a magnificent lighting arc, draped with flowers, bunting, and the symbol of the Patriotist Party, a screaming eagle.

"Faces down!" Cara hissed suddenly.

They all studied their boots. Before Dan averted his eyes, he caught sight of Galt backslapping his way through a crowd of reporters. "Welcome to our island," he told one. "Glad you could be here to help us make history," he said to another.

"Like he's going to be copresident," Dan muttered when the coast was clear.

"He can't help it," Cara reluctantly defended her brother. "I know what it's like to be Dad's favorite, with the keys to the kingdom dangled in front of you. It's hard to resist that kind of temptation."

"*You* resisted," Ian noted admiringly.

"I have a role model," she told him. "This kid who stood up to his mother for the good of humanity. Impressive guy."

Ian flushed, a slight smile tugging at him.

A plan was hatched. Jonah and Ian melted into the

staff manning the tech center behind the stage. Dan and Hamilton climbed the framework of the massive lighting arc, joining a dozen other maintenance workers.

Dan found a metal strut that he could tighten, and loosen, and tighten again, in order to look busy. He gazed out over the throng. There had to be a gazillion people here. The seating in front of the stage was strictly for VIPs. The rest would have to find spots on the beach or on the grass. No one would miss anything. Giant video screens and loudspeakers loomed all over the island.

From his vantage point, he had no trouble locating Pierce's many serum-enhanced goons. They were hard to miss, even in a huge crowd. Besides being big and ripped, they seemed to glow with an inner light — a kind of presence that could not be overlooked. And Cara was right — there were a lot of them. Easily a hundred, probably more.

Dan's face darkened as he thought of his sister. She had the glow — and also the tremors and blackouts that went with it.

Amy had the means to save herself. Yet she refused to use it until she'd delivered the antidote to Pierce Landing. The question remained: Would she have the time to get it here before her looming fate caught up to her?

CHAPTER 25

The posted start time of the All-American Clambake was three o'clock. According to the run-of-show sneaked to them by Cara, J. Rutherford Pierce would take center stage to make his candidacy official at three-thirty. The Cahills needed him and his goon army dosed with antidote before that could happen.

"Three-fifteen is our zero hour," Amy decided. "Everyone will be out where Jake and I can spray them before Pierce has a chance to open his big mouth."

"Hold on," Atticus said, "there's nothing in the antidote that can stop him from running for president. What if he makes the announcement anyway?"

"Then his enhancement will be gone," Amy replied readily, "and even his goons will be ordinary muscleheads. He can run, but he won't have any chance of winning. He'll just be the candidate who said he was Superman, but turned out to be not even Clark Kent."

Working backward from that three-fifteen zero hour, estimating wind direction and the top speed of an old crop duster, Sammy and Amy calculated the biplane's departure time from the Penobscot airstrip: two-fifty.

Roslyn was fueled up and ready, the spray tanks full of aerosolized antidote. At two-forty-five, Sammy and Atticus hugged Amy and Jake—the mission team—and withdrew to watch the takeoff.

"We'll be right here, waiting for you," Atticus called, his voice quavering just a little.

Jake flashed him a thumbs-up filled with the confidence no one felt.

Amy and Jake's final walk to the cockpit was maybe fifty yards but seemed much farther. The tremors in Amy's right leg gave her a pronounced limp, but her focus was absolute.

There was only one remaining distraction, a single detail that needed to be taken care of before she could give herself over entirely to the operation.

She gestured in the direction of the Penobscot home. "Jake—look!"

And when he turned to see what had caught her attention, she clasped her hands together and brought them down hard on the back of his neck. He hit the tarmac and lay there, stunned.

She allowed herself just an instant of regret. Nobody else saw her the way Jake did—not as a living, breathing command-and-control center, but as a sixteen-year-old girl. And how had she rewarded him? By knocking him unconscious.

Still, it had been the right thing to do. Jake had his

whole future ahead of him, and it was a brilliant one. He shouldn't have to pay with his life for his devotion to her.

She ran to the biplane, hopped up to the cockpit, and slammed the door. She started the engine, which drowned out the cries of protest coming from Sammy and Atticus. As the propeller picked up speed in front of her windscreen, she taxied out onto the strip and began to accelerate into her takeoff run.

Suddenly, there was thud against the fuselage of the biplane. The passenger door was wrenched open, and there was Jake, scrambling along the runway, trying to haul himself into the seat.

"Let go!" she shouted. Her voice enjoyed a serum boost, too.

"No!"

She never would have believed him capable of what he did next. As *Roslyn*'s front wheel left the tarmac, Jake hurled himself in through the hatch, landing upside-down in the seat. He righted himself, slamming the door behind him just as the crop duster took to the air.

"What did you hit me for?" he demanded.

"I was trying to save your stupid life!" she shot back.

He was enraged. "You want to do this alone, and *I'm* the one who's stupid?"

"I *have* to go! It's *my* family — *my* responsibility! Why would you put your life on the line for this?"

Jake glared at her as they gained altitude. "If you

have to ask me that, Amy, then you don't know me very well!"

She stared at him—this handsome teenager, who was not even officially her boyfriend, yet seemed determined to follow her to the ends of the earth.

"If it didn't say Rosenbloom on your passport," she told him, "I'd swear you were a Cahill."

"Keep your eyes on the road," he advised her.

The biplane banked east, heading for the Atlantic. Amy blinked, trying to disperse the fireworks and sunbursts that filled her field of vision. This was no time for hallucinations! She gritted her teeth and concentrated on the landmarks she knew were really there—farms sectioned into geometric shapes, the curling ribbons of roads, the rocky coast giving way to sparkling water.

The ride was hardly smooth. The engine's cry filled their ears and the craft shook with a vibration Amy could feel deep inside in her vital organs. As they bore down on the shoreline, a relentless headwind kicked up, buffeting the crop duster's nose this way and that. Weighed down by seven hundred gallons of liquid cargo, it was like flying through molasses, not air.

Jake's attention was on his watch. "Can't this thing go any faster?" he complained, shouting to be heard over the motor. "We haven't even passed over the beach yet."

"We didn't allow enough time for wind resistance," Amy called back anxiously. "I hope we're not too late. If Pierce goes indoors after his speech, the antidote might not reach him!"

Then something happened that made her forget her nervousness at the possibility of missing her shot at Pierce. The interior of the crop duster around her disappeared and she was completely surrounded by boiling walls of lava. There was no heat, but the magma prison was closing in on her. . . .

"*Amy!!*" The voice seemed to be coming from a long way off.

The next thing she knew, she was back in the cockpit. She was aware of the free-fall sensation in her stomach, that roller-coaster feeling. Jake was shaking her by the shoulders. "Wake up, Amy! Pull out of it!"

"Pull out of what?" Her own voice sounded reedy in her ears.

A glance through the windscreen answered her question. Instead of blue sky, the rock-bound coast of Maine was screaming up at her at dizzying speed.

She heaved back on the yoke in a desperate bid to bring the craft out of its dive. The biplane resisted, shaking violently as it hurtled toward the ground.

Hanging on to the controls for dear life, Amy reached down deep within herself—all the way back through the centuries to Gideon. The yoke began to move, slowly at first, and with much protesting and groaning. The shore swung away, to be replaced by the sea, and finally, the horizon.

She heaved a sigh of relief, which ended in a sharp intake of breath when she glanced over at Jake. He was ashen. In his trembling hands he held a syringe of cloudy liquid. Antidote.

"What do you think you're doing with that?" she asked harshly.

"I got Sammy to make an extra dose. You have to take it, Amy."

"And I will," she promised. "When we're done."

He would not back down. "How do you know that what just happened wasn't your last warning, and the next time, you won't wake up again?"

He thrust the syringe at her arm.

"No!" The serum made her so much stronger than him, and so much faster, that the hypodermic was bashed out of his hand even before he expected her resistance. It sailed over the seats and landed with a clink somewhere in the back of the plane.

He was almost insane with rage and grief. "What did you do that for? You just killed yourself! And there's no way I can save you!"

"You think I want to die?" she cried. The truth was that the closer she got to the end, the more acutely she felt everything she'd be giving up. It wasn't just a funeral; it was the prom she'd never attend, the brother she'd never watch grow up. . . .

With resolute effort, she forced away those awful thoughts by concentrating on her flying.

Poor Jake, she reflected. He had no idea that the stakes were now so high that the fate of one teenage girl didn't amount to anything at all.

CHAPTER 26

"Stay tuned for coverage of a CNN Live Event. We bring you to the private island of Pierce Landing, thirty miles off the coast of Maine, for an event billed as the All-American Clambake. . . ."

Fiske Cahill sat up in an easy chair in his Manhattan apartment. "It's begun, my dear," he called, the nervous edge clear in his voice.

Nellie joined him from the kitchen. She picked up the remote and began flipping channels. The clambake was on everything but Nickelodeon.

"Pierce may be a demented megalomaniac," Fiske commented, "but he certainly knows how to throw a party. There must be two thousand people there."

The island was a natural jewel clad in red, white, and blue in the sparkling expanse of the Atlantic. Yet even more striking than the beauty of the setting was the air of vitality and power. Something extremely important was about to happen on that stage. If Pierce's aim had been to focus attention on his announcement, he had succeeded beyond his wildest expectations.

Nellie moved closer to the screen, scanning the sky over this magical place.

No sign of the plane. At least, not yet.

Dan and Hamilton were at the top of the lighting arc, on a narrow access catwalk, when the ceremony began. It was more like the Academy Awards than a political rally. It would have been pretty cool to have this inside view of it, if Dan hadn't been so nervous about what they were trying to pull off.

The VIP seats were filled with celebrities. The Cahills had become used to Jonah and his red-carpet lifestyle, but never could Dan have imagined so many famous faces packed into one place. The singers who performed the national anthem had won fourteen Grammys between them. A four-star general served as emcee. They all took turns coming onto the stage to declare support for the Patriotist Party and J. Rutherford Pierce — war heroes, movie stars, dignitaries, athletes, Nobel laureates, and luminaries from every imaginable field of human endeavor.

Hamilton leaned over. "Is that what this whole thing is going to be?" he whispered in amazement. "A bunch of big shots lining up to say nice things about that creep?"

Dan nodded tensely. "Too bad we didn't bring a lie detector."

"Wouldn't help," Hamilton decided. "They have no idea how evil he is. They honestly think he's going to be the next face on Mount Rushmore."

A Medal of Honor winner claimed that only Pierce could restore America's glory after the weak bumbling of the current president. A chess master with an IQ of 212 swore that Pierce once beat him in eleven moves. The CEO of a multinational corporation got so emotional that he actually burst into tears. The message was always the same: *The country is in terrible shape; the world is falling apart. Only one man can save us: Pierce. Pierce! PIERCE!!!*

Dan caught the worried looks from Ian and Jonah at the tech station below. Ian was tapping his wrist where a watch would be. Dan shrugged helplessly. No sign of the plane.

Dan spotted the source of Ian's urgency. In the family box where the candidate himself sat with his wife, daughter, and son, bathing in torrents of praise, Cara was signaling Ian with three fingers. Could that mean three minutes before Pierce's announcement? Once he completed the transformation from Citizen Pierce to Candidate Pierce, he'd be in a cocoon of media and Secret Service. They'd never reach him then!

Come on, Amy! Where are you?

Dan forced down his dread that something even worse had gone wrong, and concentrated on the race against time. Cara was down to two fingers. Two minutes to go.

"What's going on?" Hamilton hissed. "Are we running out of time?"

Cara held up one finger. Sixty seconds!

". . . and that's how J. Rutherford Pierce brought down a twelve-point buck with a homemade crossbow. In these days of paper shufflers and talk-show phonies, what we need in the Oval Office is a *real man*!"

It got an enormous ovation.

"Thank you, Senator," the four-star emcee called jovially. "And now we've come to the highlight of our afternoon — besides a hundred thousand pieces of quality seafood, that is." Waves of laughter. "It's time to hear from the man himself —"

Cara dropped her last finger. They were out of time.

"The most successful businessman in the history of American media —"

Frantic, Dan began to unscrew one of the heavy spotlights. If he dropped it on the dais, surely they would have to postpone the proceedings long enough to sweep up the broken glass. It wasn't a great plan, but it was the only one that came to mind.

"The next president of the United States —"

A blue-coveralled figure vaulted up onto the stage from the rear. With a flourish, the newcomer shed his jumpsuit and ripped off his mustache to reveal hip-hop's biggest star, the legendary Jonah Wizard.

Jonah snatched the microphone from the emcee's hand and bellowed, "Wassup, Pierce Landing? *The Wiz is in the house!*"

CHAPTER 27

Fiske was on his feet in front of the TV. "What on earth is Jonah doing? This wasn't part of the plan!"

"He's stalling for time!" Nellie shrilled. "Look—the Piercers don't know what to make of him!"

There was an element of confusion in the cheer that greeted the superstar's arrival. This wasn't exactly a hip-hop crowd, and Jonah Wizard was nowhere on the long list of celebrities who were to attend the clambake.

The broadcast cut to a close-up of the Pierce family box. The candidate himself was under tight control, although his face seemed to be glowing a little more than usual, and there was a vein throbbing in his temple. He kept a fatherly arm on his son, Galt, who looked like he was about to rush the stage and commit murder.

"Legit, I've got some things to tell you about my man, J-dog," Jonah harangued the crowd. "Not too many people understand how respected he is in the hip-hop community. You know the expression 'like a boss'? Well, that was invented just for him, yo. And wait till you hear about *this*—"

"Uh-oh." Nellie was worried. "He's got absolutely nothing to say. He loves Pierce about as much of the rest of us."

"The Janus have the gift of gab," Fiske reminded her. "He could go on forever—but I don't think they're going to let him. Look."

A wide shot showed Pierce's serum-enhanced musclemen converging on the stage.

"And even though my record label is owned by his biggest competitor"—Jonah was floundering now—"I still consider J-dog my mentor—because—because—Wow, don't those clams smell great?"

The first of the goons climbed up on the stage and made for Jonah.

"This is bad," moaned Fiske.

Nellie's eyes were fixed on a tiny dot that had appeared in the blue sky above Pierce Landing. "That better not be a bird," she whispered.

The island lay dead ahead, but Amy Cahill was coming apart at the seams.

She clung to the yoke of the biplane like a drowning sailor hanging on to a life preserver, her arms quaking. At least her grip provided some stability. More than half of her body was completely beyond her control.

The fireworks display that distorted her vision had

only grown stronger. She squinted down at Pierce Landing through a haze of pyrotechnics, willing herself to see past the hallucinations. Big rockets roared by, missing her wings by inches, and warplanes filled the air, jockeying for position like race cars.

No! The sky is clear! I'm alone with Jake in the cockpit!

She looked over at Jake and instead found her grandmother in the other seat.

"Of course you can do it," Grace told her confidently. "You're a Cahill. You can do anything." But then, before Amy's eyes, her grandmother's serene smile twisted downward into a scowl, and she was not Grace any longer, but her older sister, Aunt Beatrice. "You're really in it now, Amy Cahill, and with no one to blame but yourself! I told you you'd end up just like your mother!"

"Amy—are you okay?" It was Jake again, no sign of Grace or Beatrice.

Even though she knew he'd been there all along, she was bizarrely glad to see him, as if he'd just come back after a two-year absence. She had a flashback to the first time she'd laid eyes on him, standing with Atticus outside the Roman Colosseum. He was gorgeous then, and he was even more gorgeous now—dark-fringed brown eyes and perfect chiseled features.

"I'm sorry about everything, Jake. You've been so great to me, and I've been so awful—"

"The plane, Amy! Fly the plane!" Jake almost screamed. "The other stuff we can talk about later!"

They approached Pierce Landing from the west.

They could see the stage and the huge crowd around it. The moment had come to ease up on the throttle. That would decrease their altitude, enabling them to cruise low over the island and spray the antidote. Her hand was on the stick, ready to cut speed.

"Amy—now!" shouted Jake.

She could not move. Of all times, of all places, her body had shut down right here. She had an oddly detached thought:

So this is what it feels like to die. . . .

"Do it!" Jake urged.

"I can't," she said, strangely calm.

"Why not?"

"My arms don't work anymore. You'll have to take over."

"What? Are you crazy?"

"You helped fly that helicopter in Tikal," she reminded him. "You can do it. I *need* you, Jake."

It might have been just her imagination, but she would have sworn he sat up a little straighter as he took the controls from her.

Amy could feel five hundred years of Cahill history guiding her every thought. Death was staring her in the face, yet she was completely focused and clear in her instructions. "See that stick on the floor? Pull it toward you . . . that's right."

Frantic with fear, Jake complied.

The crop duster swooped low over the All-American Clambake.

CHAPTER 28

The crowd had gone quiet as four of Pierce's goons climbed onto the stage and began to advance menacingly on hip-hop's biggest star.

Jonah still had the microphone. "What's the matter, fellas? Has the Wiz used up his ninety seconds?" He began to back away, but his shoe caught on an electrical cable, and he went down flat on his back. It was there, staring straight up, waiting for his field of vision to fill with enemies, that he spied the biplane. An instant later, he noticed it — a fine, cold mist descending in clouds on everything and everybody. Nothing had ever felt better. "Yo, people, is it just me or *is it raining*?"

The effect on the goons was instantaneous. The four dropped to their knees, doubled over in pain. All throughout the crowd, members of the serum-enhanced Pierce team twisted in discomfort as they breathed in the aerosolized formula that was misting down on them. In the family box, Debi Ann was the only Pierce still upright. Cara, Galt, and their father were in the throes of agony as the antidote attacked the serum in their bodies.

Throughout the crowd, a wave of confusion was cresting into hysteria. People could feel the atomized liquid coming down, could even see the clouds of vapor spewing from the wings of the plane. What was being dropped on them? Were they being poisoned? Chaos broke out across the lawns and beach as fearful spectators tried to run away, but were hemmed in by the dense crowd around them. Screams resounded. There was a stampede into the ocean as people tried to cleanse themselves of whatever it was that had rained down from the sky. And all of it was being televised and broadcast around the world by equally shocked and fearful TV reporters.

In the family box, Pierce picked himself up and gazed out over his ruined clambake. The seizure was over, but he could feel the physical reaction still churning through his body. He knew with absolute certainty what it was. Loss. Weakness. Limitation. His serum-enhanced powers were deserting him.

Those Cahill brats — Hope's children — had done it. They had perfected the antidote and found a way to deliver it. His eyes turned skyward to the crop duster, which was making a second pass. Worse, they had accomplished this while the eyes of the entire planet were upon him.

Well, it wouldn't work. He still had a small stockpile. He'd find another lab and replicate it! This was nothing more than a temporary setback. He was J. Rutherford Pierce, media tycoon and front-runner for the presidency!

He ran out onto the stage, somewhat disturbed that his stride wasn't quite as masterful as it had been a few scant minutes before. Snatching up the microphone from where Jonah had dropped it, he called, "Calm down, everybody!" Even his voice wasn't as commanding as before. "Nothing to worry about! That is just somebody's idea of a bad joke! The clambake's still on!"

It did little to restore order.

Pierce tried a different tack. "You came here to see our country take the first step on the road back to greatness. It all starts with an important announcement. Well, I'm ready to make that announcement right now!"

He looked out over the turbulent crowd. Pandemonium reigned. People were running for cover, under trees, under tables and chairs. There were fistfights over tablecloths that could be used for protection. A huge migration was in progress toward the marina, where the waiting boats bobbed. Choosing the next president was no longer high on the list of priorities.

And in the midst of this debacle, the last person he wanted to deal with came up to embrace him.

"Rutherford—you poor dear!" Debi Ann blubbered to her husband. "It's all ruined! What are we going to do with a hundred thousand clams?"

He was instantly enraged. Even in the middle of a disaster of colossal proportions, leave it to his useless, dizzy wife to seize on the only part didn't really matter. "The *clams*?" he roared. "I'll tell you what we can do with the clams! I'm going to shove them, one by one, up your nose into your empty head! Shells on!" He pushed her away with such force that she fell to the stage.

Lying flat on her back, she grinned up at him with such diabolical glee that it left no doubt she'd provoked him on purpose. Heart sinking, he turned to face the news cameras. Every single one showed a red light. His bullying of his wife had been broadcast around the world.

The American people tolerated a lot from their leaders, but *never* would they vote for a man who was low enough to mistreat his wife. Pierce would never be president. He'd be lucky to get elected dogcatcher.

Debi Ann laughed a cruel laugh. "This is for Letitia Tyler!"

Jonah Wizard reached down and helped her to her feet.

She smiled at him. "Thank you, Jonah."

"No problem, yo."

The words had barely left Jonah's lips when he spied a furious Galt bearing down on him like a charging rhino.

The crop duster lurched as the last of the antidote misted down over Pierce Landing and the wind-driven spray mechanism shut itself off.

In the cockpit, Amy was still slumped in the pilot's seat, unable to move her arms or legs. Jake was crammed into the tiny space between the chairs, leaning half around and half over her to reach the controls. But nothing could spoil the sense of triumph in the biplane. They had dispersed their payload over the clambake. From the sky they had no way of knowing what effect the antidote was having. But the turmoil down there was evident, with waves of people running in all directions.

"You did it, Amy!" Jake's voice was husky with emotion.

"*You* did it," Amy amended.

"All I did was exactly what you told me. Without you, it never could have happened. And I'm not just talking about today. All this impossible stuff lands in your lap, and somehow, you get it done. There's no one like you, Amy Cahill. . . ."

Suddenly, Jake was overwhelmed by a feeling that he was talking to himself. "Amy?"

He leaned forward and twisted to get a look at her. Her eyes were closed; she was deeply unconscious. Faint breath was coming from her nostrils, but that was as much life as he could find.

Oh, no! Amy — no!

He'd known this moment would be coming, but

nothing could have prepared Jake for the jolt of fear that tore through him.

The drive to save her overcame every urgency, even the need to fly the plane. He propped Amy's limp body against the yoke in an attempt to keep the crop duster's altitude steady. Then he scrambled behind the seats in a frantic search for the syringe she had knocked out of his hand.

For a shattering instant, it was nowhere. Then he spied it, wedged between the base of the pilot's chair and a fire extinguisher. He snatched it up, jammed the needle into her upper arm, and pressed the plunger, draining the contents into the muscle tissue.

"Wake up, Amy!"

There was no response.

"Come on! Stay with me!" He shook her, but she was dead weight.

He was so wrapped up in the drama that it took a moment for him to notice that the cockpit had tilted forward. With strength he didn't even know he had, he heaved Amy into the passenger seat and took her place at the controls. As he had seen her do, he pulled back on the yoke in a last-ditch attempt to stabilize the plane.

"*Up! Up!*" he screamed at the whirling propeller in front of him.

Icy fear clutched at his belly as he realized that the crop duster was going to crash.

All Jonah could do was cover his famous face and prepare for the onslaught of Galt's rage.

A large figure swung down from the catwalk above, riding on a bundle of electrical cables. Hamilton Holt took out Galt with a flying double-kick, knocking him across the platform and over the apron. Galt landed in the first row of seats, dazed.

Jonah looked on in admiration. "Cuz—that was OG!"

"Cara!" Ian made his way to the Pierce box, where Cara was holding on to the arms of her chair, trying hard not to slide off to the floor. "Are you all right?"

She nodded bravely, but her expression was pained. "I didn't think it was going to be so hard," she said faintly. "I've been off the protein shakes for a week."

He helped her out of the box to where Dan had joined Hamilton and Jonah.

Pierce took in the spectacle of his strong and brilliant daughter standing with the hated Cahills. His mind wasn't as sharp as it had been before the antidote, but this wasn't difficult to figure out.

"Traitor!" he roared, and she flinched in spite of the fact that she knew she was safe.

Dan rubbed his stomach, smiling sweetly. "Are those clams ready yet? I'm starved."

"Cahill punk!" Pierce spat. "You think you've won? All you've done is bust up a beach party!"

"You can't touch us now," Dan retorted. "Not with the whole world watching!"

"Don't flatter yourself," Pierce seethed. "You and your cousins are like ants — I can stomp you out at my leisure. The kind of mayhem I can unleash is beyond anything your puny mind can imagine. And then the American people will see how much they need J. Rutherford Pierce!"

Cara understood even better than the others that her father did not bluff. "What does that mean?"

The line of inquiry never got further than that. The goons who had rushed Jonah had recovered, and one of them had a headlock on Hamilton. But these were no longer the serum-enhanced henchmen who'd been training on "protein shakes." They were ordinary bodyguards now, and not even that, as their systems were shocked and weakened by the antidote. Hamilton shrugged the first man away and flattened a second with an open hand to the chin. The third reached for Dan, who danced deftly out of range and then stomped so hard on the man's foot that he doubled over in surprise and pain. The last made a run at Cara. Ian, who considered American football uncivilized, knocked the man's legs out from under him with a tackle that could have starred in an NFL training film.

"Where's Pierce?" Dan called, scanning the riot that roiled all around them.

"There!" Hamilton pointed. The would-be president was scurrying away from the ruins of the clambake in the direction of the mansion.

"Follow him!" Cara exclaimed. "Last night he was talking about big things in small packages. I've got a really bad feeling about what that might mean."

Without Amy to instruct him, Jake's pilot skills amounted to zero. The only thing he knew, by instinct alone, was to try to keep the biplane's nose up. If they went into a straight dive, they would be killed on impact. But if they could come in flat — skim the waves and then belly flop — they might have a chance.

His muscles screamed in pain from the effort of pulling back on the yoke.

He gave the unconscious Amy a play-by-play. "We're coming in hard, so if you're considering waking up, now would be a great time!"

Why hadn't she responded to the antidote? The growing lump in his throat told him there was only one reasonable explanation — that he'd given her the injection too late, and he was talking to a dead girl.

The water was no more than twenty feet below him. He had lost track of the island and couldn't break his concentration by looking for it. He hoped the mission had been successful, but right now the only mission of any consequence was staying alive.

A sudden downdraft brought them within ten feet. Or less! That sound—was it the landing gear splashing in the swells?

The impact, when it came, was monumental. It felt more like bouncing off concrete than a soft landing on water. On the recoil, Jake's head whacked against the instrument panel. His vision began to darken.

No! he thought, and bit his tongue until it bled just to keep himself awake. If he allowed himself to black out, they would both surely drown.

The biplane jounced across the water as if a giant had skipped it like a stone. The propeller stopped spinning and snapped. The wings sheared free of the fuselage, the pilot's-side door tore away, and the ocean came pouring in on them. One moment they were hanging precariously still afloat; the next they were going down fast.

The water was ice cold. Jake's pulse raced, which made holding his breath nearly impossible. But he knew he had to get Amy out of the sinking crop duster. He grabbed her around the midsection and wrestled the two of them free of the cockpit.

In horrified dismay, Jake felt her limp body slip from his grasp. He dove after her, reaching frantically.

His fingers brushed against something solid. Driftwood? A fish?

No—human skin!

He clamped hold of Amy's wrist and pulled for the surface, kicking with an effort that was nothing short of maniacal. They broke through into the sunshine, and he drew in great gulps of air. Amy gurgled and coughed up water, but did not regain consciousness.

Turning amid the swells, he scanned the horizon. Hope drained from him when he located Pierce Landing. It had to be a mile away, probably more. He wasn't sure he could swim that far himself, much less towing an unconscious girl.

He was treading water, supporting Amy Red Cross-style, when something big bumped him from behind. His mind reeled with images from *Jaws*—could a shark add anything to the disaster that had already befallen them? But when he confronted his attacker with nothing more than one fist to fight with, he found himself facing the crop duster's large payload tank.

It must have broken free when the fuselage came apart, Jake thought in wonder. *The plane sank, but the empty tank floated to the surface!*

However it had happened, he was grateful. He draped Amy across the top of the dull metal. It bobbed a little and stabilized.

He established a solid handhold, pried off his shoes, and began to kick for shore.

Cara threw open the door of the residence, ushering Ian, Hamilton, Jonah, and Dan ahead of her. "Dad!" she exclaimed. "Where are you, Dad?"

There was no reply. The mansion echoed like a barn.

"He's in here somewhere," said Hamilton. "How hard can it be to find him?"

Jonah looked around. "I knew a record producer with a crib this big. His kid's pet rabbit got loose, and it took three months to track it down."

"Let's split up and search the house," said Ian.

"But watch yourselves," Cara added. "All his plans are coming apart, and we already know he's not afraid to kill!"

That was when Dan saw it — a strip of light beneath a closed door in the hallway that led out to the garden and the pool. "What's in there?" he asked Cara in a low voice.

"Sauna and Jacuzzi," she replied.

Dan marched up and tried the knob. It was locked.

"Come on, Dad. Let us in," Cara called.

No answer.

"I got this!" Hamilton took a running start and plowed shoulder-first into the door. He bounced away as if he'd hit solid rock.

"Back off, everybody." Cara pulled a bobby pin out of her long blond hair, twisted it straight, and inserted it into the lock. "Be careful. He could be armed." After a few seconds of probing, there was a click and the door swung wide.

Ian tried to move protectively in front of her, but she brushed him aside. "I'm going first. He's my father."

Whatever defensive moves or counterattacks they feared, no one expected what they encountered inside the sauna room. J. Rutherford Pierce sat alone on the edge of the marble hot tub. He seemed not to notice them, so focused was he on the tablet computer resting on his knees.

"What are you doing, Dad?" she asked in a voice that was not unkind and even betrayed some regret.

"Don't call me that. You're not my daughter. You think you've stopped me? I'm already on my way back to what I used to be. I had the first shake a minute ago!"

Cara shook her head almost apologetically. "Ovaltine. The serum's gone, Dad. I spilled it into the Atlantic last night. Yours, the staff's — every drop."

His eyes bulged. "You were going to live in the White House. You would have been my most trusted adviser. My heir."

Her face, fair like his, radiated sincerity. "I couldn't

let you do it. One day you're going to look back and see what a crazy, twisted plot this was—with that awful serum at the heart of it."

Pierce's face twisted into a cruel scowl. "My plan will still come to pass, I promise you that. Maybe I won't win this election, thanks to your meddling. But there are other ways to show the American people that they need me!"

"You're bluffing!" Dan accused.

"We'll know in"—he consulted the tablet in his lap—"seven minutes."

A tense quiet descended. What was he talking about?

Cara had gone ghostly white. "The 'big things in small packages'?" she prompted in a small voice.

Some of the glow returned to Pierce's cheeks. "It was originally part of my campaign strategy, but it's even more perfect now that the clambake has fallen apart. I've got six small nuclear devices hidden in suitcases planted in cities around the world. When they go off, half the planet will be at each other's throats. Americans will forget about today and beg me to lead them through the perilous times ahead."

"Nuclear?" Dan was horrified. "You're going to kill millions to help make you president?"

"Just thousands," Pierce amended. "The nukes are small. The body count isn't what's important; it's the unrest that's created when all these foreigners start blaming each other."

The Cahills exchanged agonized glances. The images whirling around their minds were ghastly and appalling. Flashes of detonation; walls of flame roaring down crowded streets, incinerating everything in their path.

Not only was Pierce deranged enough to conceive of such an abominable plan, he was absolutely dead set on seeing it through.

Hamilton snatched a towel from the bar and flung it at Pierce, wrapping it around his head. As Cara's father struggled to free himself, Ian snatched the tablet from his hands.

Pierce just laughed. "You think you can stop me with that? Once the detonation sequence begins, only the abort code can stop it. My software can't be hacked. It was designed by April May herself!"

"*I'm* April May, Dad!" Cara exploded. "When I wrote that software, I had no idea you were going to use it to—" She began to sob.

He looked at his daughter, eyes widening in shock and disbelief. Then his features hardened into a mask of pure hatred.

Ian held up the tablet for the others to see. The countdown timer read 5:17.

The intense cold was beyond anything Jake could have imagined—like thousands of bee stings applied simultaneously to the entire surface area of his body. It made his muscles cramp and his heart race, accelerating the crippling fatigue that took hold in his gut and radiated outward.

He kicked through the waves, pushing the empty spray tank that carried Amy's unconscious body. His chest was so contracted with tension and effort that it hurt to wheeze in the tiniest breath. His legs were on fire, but not the kind that offered any warmth. He could no longer feel his hands.

"Hang in there, Amy," he panted. "You're going to make it."

She was still unconscious. The encouragement wasn't for her. It was a reminder for himself—why he had to wrestle the sea and the agony of his own body. She stood no chance at all if he couldn't get her to shore.

Floundering, he tried to estimate his progress. Pierce Landing still seemed impossibly distant. He couldn't tell how far he'd come, since his starting point had no marker. The wreckage of the crop duster had long since sunk out of sight.

"I don't think we're getting anywhere," he rasped aloud.

Amy had no opinion. Waves licked at a dangling strand of her long hair.

It took a moment for the importance of this to sink in. Her hair hadn't reached the water before.

The tank sat low in the swells. Tiny bubbles cascaded to the surface.

It's letting the ocean in.

The thought that followed was even more alarming: *It's going to sink!*

He began to swim with renewed vigor, kicking through the pain. He was no longer just battling the sea and the distance. He was battling time as well. Pretty soon, the tank would lose buoyancy and head for the bottom. He had to get Amy to safety before that happened.

The pain no longer mattered. He felt it, but it was irrelevant. He lost sight of the antidote, the clambake, Pierce, the Cahills, Atticus — even himself and Amy. The scope of his thinking narrowed to two words: *Keep moving.*

He could see the hulking form of Pierce's mansion and, beyond it, the lighting arc of the clambake stage. He seemed to be approaching the island's opposite shore. It was closer now, but not close enough — not nearly. The seven-hundred-gallon container grew heavier as it filled, listing dangerously to one side.

He watched in horror as the tank tipped over and sank out of sight with a gurgle and an eruption of bubbles. Amy bobbed in the ocean a moment and then disappeared beneath the surface. It was all Jake could do to gather her into his arms and pull her up again.

There was no question of a Red Cross carry. He was completely out of gas. The choice before him was cruel and starkly simple: *He* might be able to make it. But not with Amy.

It should have been an easy decision: Saving two lives was impossible; preserving one was preferable to none. Yet he could not bring himself to let go.

The Rosenblooms were long on brains. Dad, a renowned scientist; Atticus, a straight-up genius; Jake, no slouch himself. So why was he unable to accept this basic math—that one was greater than zero?

Maybe it was this: He would never be ready to give up on Amy. It was a stupid, pointless, self-destructive way to feel, but it was all he could offer her now.

He floated there, exhausted, his mind losing focus, growing numb. And he was so cold. . . .

Blackness replaced what had once been vision. Frigid ocean closed over his head. He was sinking, but he was too tired to care. A distant cry reached him, but he paid no attention, certain that it was not real.

Surely you hear things right before you die. . . .

Suddenly, he was breaching the surface, genuinely shocked to taste another breath. How had it happened? Certainly not by his own power—

Someone was beside him. It was *Amy*—kicking and paddling, dragging him up! And that meant . . .

"You're alive!" he blurted in amazement.

Incapable of an answer, she lifted one arm out of the water and pointed toward Pierce Landing.

Side by side, the two began to stroke for shore.

CHAPTER 31

Cara's nimble fingers danced over the tablet, her expression becoming increasingly tense. The count-down timer had passed four minutes. "It's no use," she breathed. "There's no way in without the abort code. I created the security myself."

Pierce offered a bitter chuckle. "That's my girl. You may be a filthy turncoat, but at least you do quality work."

"Come on, Dad," Cara wheedled. "Give me the pass-word. We're talking about *nukes* here!"

"Great leaders have to be willing to make great sacrifices," her father said righteously.

"Fine," Dan snapped. "If he won't tell us, we'll have to guess it. If I was a bloodthirsty, stuck-up, pompous nut job, what would I choose for a password?"

Pierce flamed red. "How dare you—"

"His name!" Ian interrupted. "Try his name!"

Cara was already typing: RUTHERFORD.

Invalid Code.

She tried other variations: JAMES . . . PIERCE . . . JRPIERCE . . . PIERCEJR . . .

Invalid Code.

PATRIOTIST . . . PIERCER . . . PRESIDENT . . .

Invalid Code.

"Not even close." Pierce seemed to find this highly amusing. "In fact, you're getting colder."

"What about the serum?" Dan urged as the timer ticked below three minutes. "That's what made his plan possible!"

SERUM . . . PROTEINSHAKE . . .

Invalid Code.

"Try his company!" Hamilton suggested.

FOUNDERS . . . TRILON . . .

Invalid Code.

There was the sound of running feet in the house, and a distant voice called, "Dan!"

"Amy—in here! The sauna room in the back hall!"

A moment later, Amy and Jake sloshed in through the door, sopping wet, bedraggled, and utterly spent.

Dan gawked at his sister, alive and—a blaze of relief streaked through him—could it be that she wasn't quite so juiced? "Are you—?"

"I took the antidote," she explained briskly. "But we owe the Penobscots one crop duster. *Roslyn* didn't make it." Her eyes fell on Pierce, still perched on the edge of the Jacuzzi. "What's going on here?"

The group began babbling at the same instant. Amy tuned everyone out except her brother. The two were so much on the same wavelength that she understood him instantly, half by language and half by personal radar. "It's serious, Amy!" he exclaimed. "Thousands of people are going to die!"

"So glad you'll be here to taste defeat alongside your Cahill relatives," Pierce sneered.

Cara was still typing possible passwords at light speed.

"Relatives, yo!" Jonah croaked. "Try your family!"

GALT . . . CARA . . .

Invalid Code.

"Two minutes," Ian quavered, eyes widening.

DEBIANN . . .

Invalid Code.

Pierce laughed out loud. "As if I'd use your insipid mother for anything important. She was never my first choice."

Dan stiffened like a bloodhound picking up a scent. "Amy—he was in love with Mom!"

For the first time, Pierce stopped smiling.

Amy crouched beside Cara. "Try *Hope*."

Invalid Code.

"Hope Cahill!" Amy urged as Cara pounded the touchscreen. "Or our father's last name—Hope Trent!"

Invalid Code.

"One minute!" shrilled Ian.

"We're out of time!" Jonah almost wailed. "What else, yo? Think!"

But Amy could tell from the stricken look on Pierce's

face that they were close. "Dan — what was Mom's middle name?"

He was practically hysterical. "I don't remember! Maybe I never knew! Try Grace!"

HOPEGRACE.

Invalid Code.

"Thirty seconds!" Ian squeaked.

They tried family names: HOPEANNE . . . HOPEMARY . . . HOPEELIZABETH . . .

Invalid Code.

Dan was losing it. "For God's sake, Amy, we recovered a lost antidote from a five-hundred-year-old book, but we can't come up with our own mother's middle name?"

"Ten seconds!"

Light dawned on Amy. "The *book*!" She snatched the computer away from Cara and typed: HOPEOLIVIA.

There was no response from the tablet, and for a horrible instant, Amy wondered if the screen might have frozen. Then a ping sounded and a message appeared:

DETONATION ABORTED
SYSTEM RESET

The countdown clock was halted at 0:02.

J. Rutherford Pierce, the man who had very nearly been president, laid his head in his hands and wept like a heartbroken child.

CHAPTER 32

In the attic of Bhaile Anois in the Irish village of Meenalappa, Amy and Dan stood beside their Great uncle Fiske. Four months had passed since the clambake that had been designed to change the world and had actually changed nothing at all. Across the ocean, the United States was in the midst of a presidential campaign without J. Rutherford Pierce. The Patriotist Party had disbanded. Its one-time candidate had become a joke on late-night talk shows and a sandwich at a famous Boston deli. The Pierce: bologna and Limburger on a Kaiser roll, hold the mayo and your nose.

It was amazing how quickly a global titan had morphed into a global laughingstock. But to Amy and Dan, there would never be anything funny about the media tycoon who had harnessed the power of the serum and had very nearly achieved world domination. Cahill sources inside the military had recovered the six "small" suitcase nukes from cities around the world. According to Sammy, who personally disarmed them, each bomb would have leveled a city block, contaminating a wide area with dangerous radiation. Every time Amy shut her eyes, she saw the countdown clock on Pierce's tablet: 0:02. It had been that close.

Amy was completely back to her old self. So was everybody the serum had touched.

For her part, Amy was thrilled to be ordinary again. She did not miss her superstrength and acuity—and certainly not the tremors and hallucinations that had come with the package. Best of all, zero side effects had been exhibited by anybody, including the clambake attendees who had breathed in the aerosolized spray. The antidote had lived up to the promise hidden in the cryptic poem in Olivia's book. It had taken Leonardo da Vinci and the collective knowledge of seven lost civilizations to invent it. But five centuries later, the stuff had come through with flying colors.

There was no official ceremony for what the Cahills had journeyed to Ireland to do. But it felt right to return Olivia's book to the family's ancestral home.

"Should we say something?" Dan asked in a hushed tone. "I mean, Olivia figured out a way to stop a madman who wasn't even born until five hundred years after she was already gone. If that doesn't count as clutch, I don't know what does."

"We don't have to," Fiske assured him. "You've just said it all." He wrapped the ancient book in its cloth and sealed it back in the metal box.

Amy replaced it inside the false drawer in the wooden filing cabinet. She hesitated a moment before closing it. "What if someone needs it again?"

"They won't," said Fiske firmly. "There's no more serum, and the recipe went up with the Delaware complex. Nellie and Sammy were remarkably thorough in that regard."

Dan was uneasy. Thanks to his photographic memory, he could never forget the formula for Gideon's terrible creation. As long as Dan lived, so would the possibility that the serum might return. On the other hand, he would never forget the components of the antidote, either. That was some comfort.

They left Bhaile Anois and stopped for lunch at a small teahouse in the village. Fiske took a delicate sip of his Darjeeling and sat back in his chair. "It's a shame Nellie was unable to accompany us to Ireland."

"Sammy is studying for a huge test, and she wants to be around to support him," Amy supplied. "Their relationship is getting pretty serious."

Dan made a face. "Really barfalicious is what it's getting."

"Be that as it may," Fiske said, grinning, "try to act surprised when our Nellie turns up wearing an engagement ring one of these days. Still, it is a shame she couldn't be here to share this wondrous place. It looks no different than it did in Olivia's time—unspoiled by modernity and commercialism."

He frowned as two workmen unfurled a large, glitzy poster and began pasting it to the side of a stone building in Meenalappa's central square.

"Until today," Dan put in with a grin.

"And look what it's for." Amy stifled a giggle.

The poster was a larger-than-life picture of Jonah Wizard, his microphone hand bearing the three huge, jeweled rings that had once knocked out a Pierce goon.

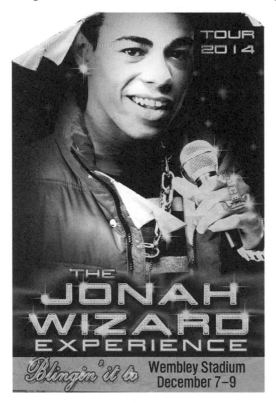

TOUR 2014

THE JONAH WIZARD EXPERIENCE

Blingin' it to Wembley Stadium December 7–9

"Dear Lord," murmured Fiske.

Dan provided the explanation. "Yeah, Jonah was

burning through his money too fast, so he decided to start touring again. Guess who his new manager is? Hamilton!"

"Hamilton *Holt*?" Fiske asked in disbelief.

"Don't sell Hamilton short," Amy advised. "He's a pretty smart guy. He doubles as Jonah's bodyguard and financial adviser. They've already bought into Debi Ann Pierce's new toy company. Supposedly, those teddy bears she makes are flying off the shelves."

Fiske nodded. "I hear she donates her share of the profits to charity."

"Yeah, she doesn't need the money," Dan agreed. "She hired a Cahill lawyer for the divorce. The guy must have been a Lucian. He took Pierce to the cleaners."

Fiske enjoyed another sip of tea and shook his head. "This is why your generation is in charge of things now. I certainly can't keep up with all that. Grace chose wisely when she chose you."

The sibling radar buzzed yet again, and Amy and Dan shared a speaking look. This was the subject they were reluctant to bring up with their great-uncle, but both realized that he deserved to know.

Amy spoke for them. "Uncle Fiske, the truth is — we're out."

The old man's eyes widened. "Out?"

"It was my idea at first," Dan admitted. "I couldn't stand what all the Cahill stuff was turning me into, and I decided that when the Pierce thing was over, I'd quit. But then Amy" — his voice caught in his throat —

"I mean, we've been in danger before, but this time it was bad. I really didn't think she'd make it."

In that moment, he resembled the eleven-year-old kid he'd been when the Clue hunt had first swept them up. Amy took his arm.

"Anyway," Dan went on, a little more steadily, "nearly losing Amy taught me that I could never leave without her. We quit together or not at all."

"Three years ago, we didn't even know what it meant to be a Cahill," Amy added. "And ever since then, we've been on a crazy treadmill with the future of humanity resting on our shoulders. We need a break. We've *earned* a break."

"Understandable," their great-uncle told them. "What will you do?"

"We'd like to travel," Amy replied evenly.

Fiske was astounded. "Travel? You've already circled the globe a dozen times!"

Dan shook his head. "This time we want to see the world without having to save it."

"Plus, we're hiding out a little," Amy admitted. "Pierce wrecked our reputation. Everybody thinks we're jet-setting spoiled brats."

Fiske's eyes twinkled. "And I suppose this has nothing to do with the fact that young Jake Rosenbloom has taken a year off his studies."

Amy blushed deep purple. "Well, we might try to — meet up — occasionally —"

His smile faded. "Only one thing concerns me. What

about the family? Who will look after Cahill affairs while you two are off on this 'break'?"

Amy and Dan exchanged a knowing glance.

"We've already thought of that," said Amy Cahill. "We've left the family in just the right hands."

A silver feline head peered off the back of an elegant Victorian chair in the old-fashioned parlor. The Cahill home in Attleboro, Massachusetts, was known as Grace's house, but there was no question that the true master of this domain was Saladin, the Egyptian Mau.

The long days spent in Aunt Beatrice's condo were finally over, and he was home where he belonged. His claws gripping the plush fabric, he raised himself just a little and set his sights on the tall dark teenager in the center of the room.

A second later, the cat was airborne, sailing past Ian Kabra's head, leaving a scratch that stretched from ear to chin.

"Ow! Saladin, you mangy refugee from a violin string factory—"

The Egyptian Mau landed softly on the carpet and tossed a defiant "Mrrrp!" over his shoulder as he made his unhurried way across the parlor.

Cara Pierce rushed in, bearing a cloth and antiseptic. A clash between Saladin and Ian was an everyday occurrence at Grace's house.

Saladin was never the one who needed first aid.

"We should get rid of that cat," Cara breathed, dabbing gently at Ian's cheek.

"We can't," said Ian, trying not to show how much he was enjoying her attention. "He comes with the house, and the house is Cahill Headquarters."

She sighed. "Then I guess he's our responsibility—along with the rest of the most powerful family in human history."

Saladin looked on in smooth indifference. He had lived here with Grace, and later with Amy and Dan. He foresaw no problems with these two.

As long as the fresh snapper kept coming.

Sirs,
The time has come
to wake the dragon.

X